THE DINGO DILEMMA

CLAIRE MCNAB

Other Bella Books by Claire McNab

Under the Southern Cross
Silent Heart
Writing My Love

Carol Ashton Series:
Lessons in Murder
Fatal Reunion
Death Down Under
Cop Out
Dead Certain
Body Guard
Double Bluff
Inner Circle
Chain Letter
Past Due
Set Up
Under Suspicion
Death Club
Accidental Murder
Blood Link
Fall Guy
Lethal Care

Denise Cleever Series:
Murder Undercover
Death Understood
Out of Sight
Recognition Factor
Death by Death
Murder at Random

Kylie Kendall Series:
The Wombat Strategy
The Kookaburra Gambit
The Quokka Question
The Dingo Dilemma
The Platypus Ploy

THE DINGO DILEMMA

CLAIRE MCNAB

BELLA
BOOKS

2020

Bella Books, Inc.
P.O. Box 10543
Tallahassee, FL 32302

First Published by Alyson Books 2006
First Bella Books Edition 2020

Printed in the United States of America on acid-free paper

ISBN: 978-1-64247-256-1

Acknowledgments

With warm appreciation for the efforts of inestimable editor, Joseph Pittman, and eagle-eyed copy editor, David Robinson. And thanks to Lisa Seidman for her invaluable input on series television.

For Sheila, my Ariana

CHAPTER ONE

"G'day," I said through the window to the bloke I'd nearly run down as I'd whizzed through the gates and into Kendall & Creeling's parking area. He moved out of the way, but didn't reply. I parked my dad's vintage red Mustang and hopped out. "Can I help you?"

Hands on hips, he was giving our building a concentrated look-see. He was a puny bloke, going bald fast, but his dark blue suit was expensive and he was wearing on his skinny wrist a Rolex watch, though it could have been a fake, for all I knew.

I joined him in his assessment of the pseudo-Spanish house that had been converted into offices. It wasn't all that long ago I'd seen it for the first time myself, having lobbed in from Australia when I inherited a controlling interest in my father's business.

The stucco walls were a bright, pinkish-ocher color, topped with a roof of fat, curved terracotta tiles. We were standing in what must have been the front garden—now a parking area.

Still without saying a word, the bloke advanced to the small tiled courtyard that led to the entrance. In the center was a little fountain I'd recently had fixed, so it was cheerfully spurting a lacy column of recycled water. The black wooden front door had many brass studs and a heavy black metal lever instead of a door handle.

"You're in need of a private eye, are you?"

That got his attention. "Private eye? Whatever gave you that idea?"

"Could be because you're standing in front of Kendall & Creeling Investigative Services."

He shook his head impatiently, then reached in his pocket, took out a silver case, opened it, and handed me a business card. "I'm a developer."

I examined the card, then stuck out my hand. "G'day, Norris Blainey. I'm Kylie Kendall."

He could hardly have been less interested. His dead-fish handshake went with his pale eyes, weak chin, and slack mouth. He dropped my fingers and went back to sizing up the property.

"It's pretend Spanish," I said.

"That doesn't interest me. As far as I'm concerned, it's a tear-down."

"A what?"

Norris Blainey sighed, mumbled something about foreigners, then said, "It'll be torn down. Demolished."

"Half a mo," I said, "no one's touching this building."

He gave me a bit of a scornful smile. "And you'd have a say?"

"I reckon so. I own it."

This was an exaggeration. Dad had left me exactly fifty-one percent of the business. His partner, Ariana Creeling, held the remaining forty-nine percent.

"You have a business card?"

"Too right I do."

I'd just had them printed, so I whipped one out and handed it to him. The company name, KENDALL & CREELING

INVESTIGATIVE SERVICES, was followed by some of the areas we covered—undercover investigations, skip tracing, surveillance, background clearances, security consulting, industrial espionage. KYLIE KENDALL appeared at the bottom right-hand corner. There was no mention, of course, that I was only a trainee PI.

Norris Blainey was looking at me with considerably more interest than before. "This section of Sunset Boulevard is ripe for development," he declared. "We'll be approaching your neighbors with offers they won't be able to refuse." With sudden enthusiasm, he flung his arms wide. "My company aims to level this entire block and build a complex of multi-level offices and condos."

"Forget about leveling Kendall & Creeling. It's not going to happen."

Seeming surprised, he said, "You can't stand in the way of progress."

This bloke was well on the way to giving me the irrits. "Just watch me."

He slapped on an ingratiating smile. "I know it feels more comfortable to resist change, but when I get back to you in writing with an offer—a very generous offer—I'm convinced you'll realize selling is to your considerable advantage."

"Write away. You'll have Buckley's."

I was about to clarify that this meant he had no chance at all, but Norris Blainey was already heading for the street. "I'll get back to you," he called over his narrow shoulder.

I shoved open the front door in a dark mood. What if all the other places along our section of Sunset Boulevard gave in and sold out to this developer bloke? What if our offices were surrounded by looming buildings, cutting out the sunshine? What if—

"Kylie!"

I focused on Melodie, seated behind the new desk Fran had ordered—a Spanish-themed black wooden number which had been artificially aged to look like something out of *Don Quixote*.

Melodie was Kendall & Creeling's receptionist, at least until her career in acting took off in a big way. "What's up?" I asked.

"Like, it's real serious." She put her hand to her throat. "*Real serious.*"

I wasn't alarmed. Melodie never missed an op to hone her dramatic skills. "Don't tell me Julia Roberts is upsetting Lonnie again. He'll have to learn to deal with it."

Melodie shook her head, swirling her long blonde hair in her shampoo-ad manner. Big green eyes wide, she said, "It's your mom. You just missed her call."

It was my turn to clutch my throat. Back in Australia, my mum ran The Wombat's Retreat hotel in Wollegudgerie, my hometown. Ever since I'd arrived in LA, Mum had been working hard to get me to return to the Outback and help her run the pub, since Jack, her fiance, had turned out to be pretty much a no-hoper in this area.

"What's happened?" I asked with foreboding. "Is she okay?"

"I guess it's real complicated. Your mom said to call her back the moment you came in."

"Give me a clue," I said. "The pub hasn't burnt down, has it?"

"Your mom said something about a tractor and a dingo."

"A tractor and a dingo?"

Melodie clasped her hands. "A dingo's got my baby!" she announced in deeply tragic tones.

I'd heard this line a thousand times while Melodie'd been practicing what she fondly believed was an authentic Aussie accent, though she wasn't within a bull's roar of one. Trying not to sound impatient, I said, "Meryl Streep in *A Cry in the Dark.* Yes?"

"Malcolm, my voice coach, says Meryl's got the accent," Melodie declared, "but not the Aussie cadence, like I have."

In my opinion, Malcolm wouldn't recognize an Australian accent if it leapt up and smacked him in the kisser, but I kept this to myself. "Any other messages?"

"Fran says to tell you the shed for the backyard's arriving tomorrow and the guys will have it up by lunchtime. She's expecting you to help shift the office supplies so she can put her disaster stuff in the storeroom."

Fran had bestowed upon herself the title of Office Manager, and since she was Ariana Creeling's niece, she was hard to challenge when she got a bee in her bonnet about something. Being of a naturally pessimistic nature, Homeland Security's dire warnings about disaster preparedness had fallen on fertile ground. Fran was accumulating a range of disaster supplies faster than we could find places to store them.

"That's bonzer," I said, not meaning it. I had plans for that storeroom, but until I could come up with somewhere else to store Fran's disaster stuff I was stymied.

Before returning Mum's call, I soothed myself with the routine of making myself tea. I heated the teapot with half a cup of hot water, emptied that out and added loose tea leaves and boiling water, waited four minutes, then poured myself a cuppa. Thus fortified, I went to my office, shut the door, picked up the phone, and punched in the number before I was tempted to find some delaying tactic to put off the moment when Mum would beg me to come home, and I'd say no.

It was very early morning in Wollegudgerie, but Mum always got up with the birds. She was more than fifteen thousand kilometers away, but she came down the line as clearly as if she were in the room with me. "Kylie, you're okay?"

"Yes, of course. Why wouldn't I be?"

"You're living in LA, aren't you?"

"Yes, but—"

"It's on the telly every blessed night. Freeway shootings, carjackings, serial killers—"

"Melodie said something about a dingo," I interposed, before she could whip herself into a lather.

"Not a dingo, dear. Dingo O'Rourke. You know, Harry and Gert's boy. Your cousin, a few times removed."

"What about him?" Doug O'Rourke had always been called Dingo, maybe because he was a bit like a wild dog himself.

"Harry's beside himself with worry."

"I'm sorry to hear that, Mum, but I can't see—"

"His only son, living in that hellhole called LA."

"Dingo's *here?*"

"Really, Kylie, I wish you'd listen. I've just told you that. He's landed himself a job as a dingo wrangler on some TV show."

"You don't mean *Darleen Come Home*, do you?"

When I'd heard that they were making a family show modeled on the old Lassie series, but starring a dingo instead of a collie, I'd had a bit of a giggle to myself. Fair dinkum, a dingo would be more likely to take a bite out of someone, rather than carry out a rescue.

"That's the show—*Darleen Come Home*. I don't mind telling you, Dingo's making a pretty penny working on it, but something's gone wrong."

"A problem with Darleen the dingo? She won't come home?" I said with a grin.

I'd tried to sound serious, but sharp as a tack, Mum picked up that I was amused. "This is no laughing matter, Kylie," she said severely. "Harry says Dingo's acting like he's in big trouble, but when Harry asks him what's up, he says everything's OK. I said to Harry—Harry I said, I know only too well what it's like to have one's child run off to a foreign country without a thought of the deep worry it causes a parent."

"Mum—"

"And when it's Los Angeles...well! Murder capital of the world, isn't it?"

"Nowhere close. In fact, the murder rate's falling."

Mum always ignored contrary facts. "So I said to Harry, Kylie will look into it and get back to you. No charge, of course. I mean, this is family."

I repressed a sigh. "Harry hasn't thought of coming over here himself, to see what's going on?"

"Can't. He's got to stick by Gert, seeing as she fell off the tractor and did herself a fair bit of damage. Of course it was her own fault. She was doing wheelies in wet grass, the silly chook."

"She's badly hurt?"

"A few broken bones," said Mum airily. "Nothing major, but you know how Gert loves to hold center stage. She's got Harry at her beck and call. Suits her down to the ground."

"I'm awfully busy, Mum."

"This is *family*, Kylie."

My mother had me there. There was no argument I could marshal against the family card. "OK, what do you want me to do?"

"Just find out what's wrong with Dingo. He'll talk to you. Harry and Gert will feel so much better knowing you're on the case."

I got details from her of where Dingo O'Rourke was working, the address of his apartment, and the number of his mobile phone—I reminded myself it was *cell* phone in the States.

"I'm not promising anything, Mum."

"No probs for you, darl, you being almost a private eye."

I started to say goodbye, but my mum said, "Oh, there is one more thing."

An ominous premonition swept over me. "What?"

"It's Nephew Brucie." Mum always called her sister's son "Nephew Brucie" because she knew it annoyed him mightily.

"What about him?"

"He's talked Harry into paying his airfare. He's intending to join you in LA to help with Dingo."

An involuntary cry of horror broke from my lips. "Not my cousin Brucie!"

"Millie and I tried to stop him, but it was no use."

I said goodbye, put down the receiver, then slumped in my chair. Norris Blainey was aiming to tear down the building. I had a non-paying job to find out what was ailing Dingo O'Rourke. And my noxious cousin Brucie was about to lob into LA.

Wouldn't it rot your socks?

CHAPTER TWO

I put my head around Ariana's door, hoping to find her in her office, but saw with a stab of disappointment that she wasn't there. Then I remembered she'd mentioned going to the dentist this morning, so I left a note on her desk: *Not to be a total panic merchant, Ariana, but some developer is after our building. His name's Norris Blainey and he looks to me like he's the type to pull a swifty.*

Deciding a fresh cup of tea would raise my flagging spirits, I headed for the kitchen, arriving just as Kendall & Creeling's technical wizard, Lonnie Moore, appeared.

"Doughnuts," he said. "I heard there were doughnuts." He patted his plump stomach. "Hunger," he said. "Gnawing hunger. I haven't eaten since last night."

This was hard to believe, as Lonnie was a devotee of fast food, and usually picked up breakfast from a McDonald's drive-through on his way to work.

"You missed out on McDonald's this morning?"

Lonnie gave me his charming, little-boy smile. "Well, no, but I ate practically nothing—just a couple of Egg McMuffins." He scanned the kitchen and homed in on a box labeled Delicioso Doughnuts that in my angst I hadn't even noticed. "Ah-hah!" he said triumphantly. "I thought I heard Fran telling Melodie last night she'd pick these up on the way to work this morning."

"Lonnie, have you heard of a bloke called Norris Blainey? He says he's a developer."

Lonnie was already chomping on a chocolate doughnut, so his reply was indistinct. He swallowed, sighed with pleasure, then said, "Bad news."

"Norris Blainey's bad news?"

"Ruthless. A big real estate shark. Destroys neighborhoods. Throws widows and orphans out on the street."

"Stone the crows! *That* bad?"

Having demolished one doughnut, Lonnie was busy selecting another. "Where did you run across Blainey?"

"Outside in the car park. He was giving our building the once-over."

"He was here?" For a moment Lonnie lost interest in food, which immediately indicated I had a lot to worry about. "Jesus, there goes the neighborhood."

"Norris Blainey told me he aims to buy out everyone on the block, demolish the whole shebang, and put up a complex of offices and condos."

"Bummer. We'll have to relocate."

"Kendall & Creeling's not going anywhere, Lonnie. No one's buying us out."

Lonnie looked at me gloomily. "Good luck. Blainey's a lot tougher than anyone you've met in the Outback. This guy's an operator."

"I've handled yobbos in the bar of Mum's pub who'd eat Norris Blainey for breakfast," I declared.

He shook his head so violently a lock of straight brown hair fell over one eye, giving him a rakish, devil-may-care appearance. "No way. You're totally out of your depth here, Kylie. Blainey's the developer from hell." Lonnie sighed heavily. "I don't know how I'll face relocating all my stuff. I mean, I know where everything is in my room, right now. But if I have to pack it up and move it..."

A vision of Lonnie's room swam before my eyes. It was always an indescribable mess, packed with electronic gear of every type, along with folders, papers, books, abandoned coffee mugs, and various odd items, like the knee-high gnome that had suddenly appeared one day recently. I'd asked Lonnie about it, and he'd become evasive.

I was about to bring up the gnome again—it was good practice for my interviewing skills—when I heard the unmistakable sound of Melodie tapping down the tiled hallway in her super-high heels. Crikey, I reckon I'd be tottering, not walking, but Melodie had the balance of a gymnast and titanium ankles.

"I thought so," she snapped, striding across the kitchen and snatching the box of Delicioso Doughnuts from Lonnie. "They're not all for you. If you've taken the last chocolate one, you're history, Lonnie."

"There's plenty for everyone," he said with dignity. He opened the refrigerator door and peered inside. "Who's taken my passion fruit tea?" He glared at us accusingly. "I see peach and apricot, but no passion fruit."

"Don't look at me," I said. Blimey, it was bad enough that the stuff was weak, iced tea, but to put artificial flavors in it as well? Yerks! I didn't show my disgust, as Lonnie loved to tease me about what he called my flavored-tea phobia.

"It just so happens I noticed Harriet drinking passion fruit tea," Melodie said. "She's minding the front desk for me. I bribed her with a doughnut."

Lonnie's chubby face darkened. "Pregnancy won't protect her," he said. "Harriet knows perfectly well that passion fruit's my favorite." He paused at the door to say with a helpful smile,

"If you like, I'll take the doughnuts up to her so she can choose the one she likes."

"Dream on, Lonnie. You'd eat half of them on the way."

He seemed wounded at Melodie's charge, well founded though it was. "Trust is a precious thing," he said. "Unfortunately it's in short supply around here."

"Rather like doughnuts," Melodie said pointedly to his departing back. She turned her attention to me. "Did you find out what the story was with the tractor and the dingo?"

"Nothing to do with a native dog. It's a bloke called Dingo O'Rourke. He's a distant cousin of mine and is working as a dingo wrangler on *Darleen Come Home.*"

Melodie's eyes lit up. "No! On *Darleen Come Home?* Larry-my-agent says with my mastery of an Aussie accent, I'm practically a sure thing for a part. He's lining up an audition for me as we speak."

Melodie referred to her agent so often that he'd become a hyphenated phrase in my mind. "Larry-my-agent's a bit off the mark, isn't he? The show's set in Texas."

"Sure, but there's an Australian in the cast—Dustin Jaeger. He plays Timmy, the adopted son of the Hardestie family. Aussies turn up all the time in the stories. Don't you watch it?"

I confessed I didn't. Melodie showed amazement. "But it's a *hit*, Kylie. Like everyone wants a dingo for a pet, now they've seen Darleen in action."

Whether it was fair or not, where I came from wild dingoes were regarded as sly and treacherous. "I wouldn't leave a kid alone with a dingo," I said. "You'd come back and the kid'd be gone, and the dingo'd be smacking his lips. Look what happened to the baby in *A Cry in the Dark.*"

"That was a rogue dingo," Melodie declared. "Darleen's quite different."

Lonnie came sauntering into the kitchen, attracted by the magnetic qualities of the remaining doughnuts. "Harriet says to hurry up, Melodie. She's got an appointment with her doctor. The baby's due any day now." Anxiety creased his brow. "I do hope Harriet doesn't go into labor while she's here. I'm not good with anything medical."

"No worries," I said. "You can keep yourself busy boiling lots of water while Melodie and I deliver the baby."

"I know you're supposed to have boiling water for babies being born, but what's it for?" he asked.

"It's just to keep people like you occupied, so you don't have hysterics."

Indignant, Lonnie said, "I do *not* have hysterics. The sight of blood makes me faint, that's all."

From Melodie's expression it was clear that for her, childbirth was not a gripping subject. She broke in with, "Lonnie, have you heard? Kylie's cousin is the dingo wrangler on *Darleen Come Home*. Isn't that great? It's like, a personal link to the show to know the dingo wrangler."

"Oh, yeah?" said Lonnie, not impressed. "I know a *star* wrangler."

"Oh, Lonnie, you do not"

Clearly miffed, he snapped, "Why's that so hard to accept?"

"What's a star wrangler?" I asked.

"They guarantee to deliver the right celebrity guests to events and parties," said Melodie. "Let's say you have this big function, and you want Hilary or Paris or Scarlett or Lindsay, or a power couple like Tom and Katie, then a star wrangler corrals them for you. Of course, you need celebrity bait, too."

"Appearance money," said Lonnie, in the manner of one in the know. "Gifts, publicity, donations to the star's favorite charity. All that sort of stuff."

"What's the name of this star wrangler you say you know?" asked Melodie, deeply suspicious. "You've made it all up, haven't you?"

"I've made nothing up. Pauline works for Glowing Bodies, the event coordinators."

"Glowing Bodies is the company name?" I said.

"Celebrities sort of glow, more than ordinary people," Lonnie pointed out. "So, Glowing Bodies."

"I've been told *I* have a radiance, a sort of glow about me," Melodie declared.

Lonnie unsuccessfully repressed a chortle. She glared at him. "Something's funny?"

"Not more than usual," he smirked.

"This Pauline," said Melodie, looking narrowly at him, "what's her last name?"

"Feeney. Pauline Feeney."

"She's your girlfriend?"

A blush spread over Lonnie's chubby face. "You could say that."

"I don't believe it!" She turned to me. "Do you believe it, Kylie?"

"Well, if Lonnie says so…"

Fran chose this moment to appear at the kitchen door. Obviously she was in a dark mood, which was par for the course. Fran wasn't tall but she made quite an impression, combining a spectacular bust line, porcelain skin, and dark auburn hair with the bleakest of expressions. She rather reminded me of an exquisite but malevolent doll.

"Harriet's bladder won't take any more," she announced. "She says you asked her to mind the telephone for five minutes. That was at least twenty minutes ago, Melodie. And Harriet wants to know where her doughnut is."

"Fran, what do you think of this? Lonnie says he's got a girlfriend. She star wrangles for Glowing Bodies."

Fran shot a look at Lonnie, who was still faintly pink. "A girlfriend? I don't believe it."

Seriously displeased, Lonnie snapped, "Why not?"

"Lonnie, face it, you've never mentioned a girlfriend before," Fran pointed out.

"Just because I don't parade my personal life—"

"How did you meet Pauline?" Melodie demanded. "Spell it out. At some celebrity do? I don't think so!"

Lonnie had gone quite red again. "If you must know, through a dating service. A very reputable company, Soulmate Discovery."

"A dating service? A star wrangler working for an outfit like Glowing Bodies would need a dating service?"

Stung by Melodie's incredulity, Lonnie said furiously, "Pauline says once you've got past the fame, celebrities are totally shallow and self-centered. You can't have a meaningful relationship with them, because they're all in love with themselves."

"That's true," said Fran. "Quip says the same thing."

Quip was Fran's husband, and wrote screenplays that so far had never been produced. He was a gorgeous bloke, and struck me as gay as billy-oh, but he and Fran seemed to have a happy marriage—or as happy as you could have with Fran's outlook on life.

Encouraged by Fran's support, Lonnie said with a superior smile, "Pauline says if I want to meet celebrities, she can get me an invitation to any event I like. Just name it, and I'm in."

A calculating expression flashed across Melodie's face. "Now I think about it, Lonnie, I can see why Pauline would be drawn to you when all she does is handle high-maintenance celebrities. I mean, you're just an ordinary person."

Looking quite chuffed, Lonnie said, "She does say it's great to be with someone normal."

"Or what laughingly passes for normal," Fran observed.

The phone on the kitchen wall rang. As I was nearest, I answered it. Harriet, who normally was the most even-tempered person on earth, snarled, "Put Melodie on."

"It's Harriet for you," I said, holding out the receiver.

Melodie grabbed the Delicioso box and shot out the door. "Tell her I'm on my way with doughnuts," she called back over her shoulder.

I passed on the message. "About time!" Harriet snapped.

"Lonnie," said Fran in a surprisingly sweet tone, "about tomorrow…"

He was immediately wary. "What about tomorrow?"

"We need to move the office stuff out of the storage room to make room for the disaster supplies."

"*You* need to move the stuff, not me. I'm way too busy."

Fran's near-pleasant expression vanished. "Is that so?" she said icily. "Then I'll be way too busy to provide you with essential supplies when the terrorists strike with a dirty bomb or germ warfare. Homeland Security says it's only a matter of time."

Lonnie looked stubborn.

"Or when the Big One hits, which could be any day now."

I shivered. I'd only been in LA a few months, but had already experienced a minor earthquake and lots of aftershocks. The thought of the Big One was just too horrible to contemplate.

"Countless frantic survivors," said Fran, warming to the theme, "crying out desperately for water, food, and medical equipment." She paused meaningfully. "The very supplies which I just happen to have stockpiled."

"It'll never happen," said Lonnie, without much confidence.

"Moaning in pain…"

Lonnie threw up his hands. "Oh, all right. I'll help."

Fran turned to me. "Kylie?"

"Right-oh. I'll be there."

The phone rang. It was Melodie. "Your Aunt Millie's calling. Sounds real upset. I thought you might like to take it in your office."

Hell's bells! First Mum, now Aunt Millie. A dark pessimism, worthy of Fran, swept through me. Could the day possibly get worse? I had the awful conviction that it could.

CHAPTER THREE

"My Brucie's a headstrong boy," Aunt Millie announced as soon as I picked up the phone. I could visualize her short, stocky body and grim expression—she and Fran shared the same bleak outlook on life—as she added darkly, "I know only too well what the fleshpots of Hollywood have to offer a young, impressionable fellow like Brucie. I'm relying on you to keep him on the straight and narrow, Kylie."

"Fair go, Aunt Millie! I'm on a case, so I won't have time to keep an eye on Brucie."

Aunt Millie snorted scornfully. "A case? Looking up Dingo O'Rourke is a *case?*"

Obviously Mum had told her all about Harry and Gert's worries about their son. "I'm looking up Dingo as a favor," I said, "but that doesn't mean it won't take a bit of time to check things out."

That elicited another snort from my aunt—she had a nuanced scale of such sounds, running from mild disapproval to total outrage. I pegged this one as mid-range derision. "I can tell you exactly what's wrong with Dingo. He's an idiot, silly as a two-bob watch. But then, what would you expect, with a mother like Gert O'Rourke?"

There was a long-standing feud between Aunt Millie and Dingo's mum. The reasons were lost in time, but I dimly recalled it was something to do with a recipe for lemon meringue dessert and a blue-ribbon prize for cooking at the Wollegudgerie Harvest Fair.

"When does Brucie arrive in LA?" I asked in a conciliatory tone.

"Any day now. He went off to Sydney with some of his mates for a farewell bash before he hopped on the plane."

Sydney was quite a way from my hometown, and Cousin Brucie hadn't ever traveled far from Wollegudgerie before. "His mates didn't throw him a party at the 'Gudge?"

"They knew I'd have their guts for garters if they even tried. Brucie knows my feelings—I'm totally opposed to this wild plan of his to join your PI firm."

Crushing down a yelp of deep dismay at the very thought of Brucie working for Kendall & Creeling, I said as calmly as possible, "I'm totally opposed to it, too."

"I hope you stick to that, my girl. Brucie can be a bit of a charmer, you know."

I had to repress a laugh. My cousin a charmer? He was a noxious know-it-all with all the charisma of a warthog. "I'll resist his charm as best I can," I said.

There was a knock at the door. With pleasure I saw that it was Ariana Creeling, my business partner. I gestured her into the room as I said to Aunt Millie, "Sorry, but I have to go."

"Not until I have a firm undertaking from you that you'll make sure Brucie stays out of trouble."

"Aunt Millie—"

"I'm relying on you, Kylie. Brucie is your cousin."

"Cousin or not, you know Brucie and I don't get on. There's no way he'd listen to me."

This got a reluctant grunt from my aunt. "It's true you've been at each other's throats since you were kids. Very well, then, I'm asking you to do your best. Fair enough?"

"I'll do my best, for what it's worth."

"Hmmm..."

The sound of Aunt Millie musing almost always presaged something unfortunate. "What are you thinking?" I asked with trepidation.

"I'm thinking that notwithstanding my opposition to Brucie joining your PI business, you'd find it easy to keep an eye on him if you gave him some sort of temporary position."

"No way am I giving Brucie a job at Kendall & Creeling!"

Aunt Millie tut-tutted. "There's no call for you to use that tone with me."

"I'm sorry," I said, not really meaning it.

Before ringing off, Aunt Millie pointed out she would be expecting me to provide regular reports on Brucie's activities in Los Angeles. She brushed aside my protests with, "Brucie's *family*, Kylie, and don't you forget it."

After my second daunting call from Australia in the space of a couple of hours, it was a delight to turn to Ariana. She was her always-elegant self in black silk shirt, black pants and high-heeled boots. Her pale blond hair was pulled back to emphasize the cool beauty of her face. I felt the usual pleasant jolt from her electric blue eyes.

"Help!" I said. "Save me from my relatives."

Ariana smiled. "I gather Kendall & Creeling is not about to employ your cousin, Brucie?"

"Crikey, no!"

I gave her a rundown of my earlier conversation with Mum about Dingo O'Rourke and then the gist of my chat with my aunt. Ariana had met Aunt Millie, and inquired if her son took after her.

"You mean is he mega-pessimistic, like his mum? Not at all. Brucie's the life of the party."

Actually he was a pain in the neck, but maybe he'd be on his best behavior in a foreign country. One could hope.

Pushing aside the disheartening thought of Brucie on the loose in LA, I said, "You got my note about Norris Blainey? Lonnie says he's the developer from hell."

"He is that. Blainey's been accused of numerous illegalities and shady dealings over the years, but nothing's ever stuck."

"When I met him trespassing in our parking area, he told me he was planning to demolish every building in the block and put up offices and condominiums. I didn't take him all that seriously."

Ariana leaned back in the chair, her expression grave. "This could be a real problem, Kylie. If Blainey's got plans for this area, he'll use any method, legit or not, to bulldoze the opposition."

"He's not getting his greedy little mitts on our building."

She nodded slowly. "I'm with you all the way, but I think we're in for a nasty fight. We need an attorney specializing in the field. If you agree, I'll contact Kenneth Smithson of Smithson & Wiley. He's had a lot of experience in the area, and has run into Blainey before."

"Right-oh." I smiled at her, thinking how she glowed against the somber tones of the room. This had been my father's office, and I hadn't liked to change the decor of charcoal carpet and dark gray metal furniture.

Glowed made me think of Lonnie. "Ariana, did you know Lonnie is dating a star wrangler who works for some mob called Glowing Bodies?"

"The event coordinators? Yes, I'm familiar with the company. We've done some security work for them in the past. Who's Lonnie dating?"

"Someone called Pauline Feeney. They met online."

Ariana chuckled. "Pauline's a total original and quite a handful for any man, let alone Lonnie. A few years back, she was involved in a stalking case."

"Who was stalking her?"

"No one. *She* was the stalker."

"Blimey," I said, "someone ought to warn him."

"I doubt he needs warning. At the very least he will have Googled Pauline Feeney's name. That'd bring up quite a few hits."

"He seems quite smitten," I said.

We were silent for a moment, considering the unprecedented concept of Lonnie in love. The thought dampened my mood considerably, since I was irresistibly reminded that I loved Ariana and she didn't love me.

Oh, she was fond of me, and we'd had a couple of quite spectacular sessions in bed, but that wasn't nearly enough. It was probably hopeless, but I wanted her to love me as I loved her, which was pretty well totally.

"I want the entire enchilada," I said.

Ariana raised an eyebrow. "Pardon me?"

Crikey! I'd done it again—absent-mindedly spoken my thoughts aloud. It was a habit I just had to break before it really got me into trouble. Like now.

"Dinner tonight," I said hastily, hoping my face wasn't red. "I'm thinking Mexican. Would you like to join me?"

"Sorry, Kylie, I'm not free tonight."

Not free? That made me even gloomier. Ariana was not free tonight, not free to love me…and maybe never would be.

"No worries," I said. "Julia Roberts can keep me company." It occurred to me that I hadn't seen her graceful feline self since I'd served her breakfast this morning. "You don't happen to know where Jules is, do you?"

"When I came in, Melodie mentioned she'd just seen a mouse in Lonnie's office, so she put Julia Roberts in there to catch it."

Lonnie was violently allergic to cats, so he avoided Julia Roberts whenever possible and had made it clear she was forever banned from his room. This, of course, only made Jules more determined to enter the forbidden area.

"It's a phantom mouse," I said with conviction, "created to punish Lonnie, because he laughed at Melodie when she said she had a glow about her."

"A glow?" said Ariana with a grin. "I won't ask." She got to her feet. "Let me know how you go with Dingo O'Rourke."

As she reached the door, I said, "Would you like to catch a movie this weekend?"

"Kylie..."

"Just a movie. I'm not asking for anything else."

She looked at me for a long moment, then said, "I'll get back to you."

Slightly heartened, since this wasn't an unequivocal no, I picked up the phone and tried Dingo's cell phone. He didn't pick up, so I left a brief message on his voicemail asking him to call me.

Then I went to collect Julia Roberts from Lonnie's office. Fortunately he wasn't there, as he would have been outraged at the sight of Jules comfortably ensconced in his chair, delicately balanced with one foot in the air as she washed her tawny nethers.

"Found the mouse?" I inquired.

She paused for a moment to cast me a look equivalent to an elegant shrug, then resumed her ablutions.

"You're right, Jules," I said, looking around the chaotic collection of items filling the room, "it's hopeless. There's enough cover for an entire battalion of mice. You're wasting your time here."

She protested as I scooped her into my arms and deposited her outside in the hallway. With her ears sideways in a peeved frown she watched me shut Lonnie's door, then she stalked off with an indignant snap of her tail.

Mentioning enchiladas to Ariana earlier had made me feel quite hungry, so I went up to the front desk to tell Melodie I'd spring for lunch for everyone if she'd order a delivery from the local Mexican restaurant. I found her completely absorbed, tapping away on a laptop.

Melodie hadn't noticed my approach. As she typed, her expression kept changing. One moment it was dreamy, the next vivacious. This was so intriguing I nipped up behind to get a gander at the screen.

"You love walking hand-in-hand along a beach at dusk?" I said. "And toasting marshmallows by a campfire? And dancing the night away?"

"Kylie! You gave me a fright!"

"Sorry."

Rather pink, Melodie said, "Just for a laugh, I was filling in a personality profile for a dating service. Like, everybody does it."

I peered at the laptop. SOULMATE DISCOVERY SERVICE. RESULTS GUARANTEED! appeared at the top of the Web page. "Isn't that the dating service Lonnie used to meet Pauline Feeney?"

"Could be." Melodie's embarrassed expression changed to one of entreaty. "Kylie, don't tell Fran about this, will you? Or Lonnie. In fact, don't tell anybody, OK?"

"My lips are sealed."

"Because they wouldn't understand I was just fooling around." She spread her arms wide. "I mean, look at me. Do you think I'd need help getting dates?"

I surveyed her slim figure—she was much thinner than me—her long blond hair and wide green eyes. "I reckon not."

"Of course, I don't go out with just *anyone*. I mean, I'd never date just for the sake of dating, if you see what I mean?"

"I see what you mean," I said obligingly.

"Like, I have my career to think about. Larry-my-agent says it's essential to be seen with the right people in the right places, and most vital of all—"

I never found out what this most vital thing was, because at this point the front door was flung open and a skeletal woman, accompanied by two unleashed standard poodles, one black and one white, strode in. She gestured with a hand weighed down by many rings, and the poodles obediently sat, one on either side of her.

The woman was, to say the least, an arresting figure. Her face was dead white, her lipstick brilliant red, her short hair midnight black. She had on a tight purple Spandex top and what I took to be a version of a brightly colored gypsy skirt, with many ruffles. On her feet were strappy purple sandals. Most notable of all, around her neck was a jeweled collar which exactly matched the jeweled collars her poodles wore.

"My man, Lonnie," she said in a surprisingly soft, sweet voice, "where is he?"

Melodie didn't miss a beat. "Lonnie stepped out for a moment. He'll be back soon." Flashing a dazzling smile with her perfect dental equipment, she added, "You must be Pauline Feeney of Glowing Bodies."

She nodded, then fixed Melodie with an intent gaze. "I never forget a face. I've seen you on the small screen. Refulgent Toothpaste, wasn't it?"

This was Melodie's great success story, and so far the only commercial in which she'd appeared. Melodie's smile grew even wider, exposing another couple of tooth veneers to the air. "Yes, that's right! I'm the Refulgent Girl in the Laundry."

"Your name?"

"Melodie Davenport," Melodie breathed. I happened to know her last name was Schultz, but as Melodie had pointed out, that was not the name of a star-to-be.

I came around the other side of the desk to check out the poodles. Much as I liked dogs, I did have Julia Roberts's welfare to consider. For all I knew, these two were inveterate cat chasers, and Jules could come around the corner any moment and create a nasty scene.

The white poodle was nearest to me. "G'day," I said. "How are you with superior felines?"

"That's Upton and this is Unity," Pauline Feeney said, indicating the black poodle. She added with a hint of asperity, "Both are highly trained, and are totally under my control. If they weren't, then I'd have them on leashes, wouldn't I?"

"Fair enough." I put out my hand. "Kylie Kendall," I volunteered helpfully. "You wouldn't know me from a bar of soap."

She shook my hand briefly, her very red lips curved in a faint smile. "You're too modest. You're Ariana's business partner. Brought up in some little outback town in Australia. You inherited a controlling interest in Kendall & Creeling when your father died."

Blimey, this sheila knew a lot more about me than was comfortable. Lonnie had obviously been gasbagging.

Almost as though my thoughts had materialized him, Lonnie came rushing through the door. Red and perspiring, he exclaimed, "Pauline! I saw your car, and realized you'd arrived early. So sorry I wasn't here."

"Well, you're here now," she said, taking his arm.

"Hold my calls, Melodie," said Lonnie in an authoritative tone as he and Pauline set off in the direction of his office, with Upton and Unity trotting along behind.

"Watch out for Julia Roberts," I called after them.

"'Hold my calls,' he says," muttered Melodie to herself. She gave a snort worthy of Aunt Millie. "Lonnie's just trying to impress her."

"I reckon she's going to be impressed by the state of Lonnie's office."

This thought cheered Melodie. But then her expression grew speculative. "Is it true what Pauline Feeney said—that you own more of Kendall & Creeling than Ariana does?"

"Forty-nine to fifty-one percent. Didn't you know that?"

"I never liked math," Melodie said with an airy gesture. She frowned. "No offense, but it's hard to believe you have more say than Ariana."

I knew exactly what she meant. Ariana radiated cool, controlled authority. I wasn't altogether sure what I radiated, but it wasn't that.

"What do you see when you look at me?" I asked.

Melodie frowned. "It's obvious, isn't it? I see you, Kylie."

"Imagine you were auditioning me. What would you see then?"

Melodie's expression cleared. "I get what you mean." She cocked her head, considering me. "Nice hair, much better styled than when you came, but you should consider color. I mean, dark brown is boring, don't you think? Good skin, but you've got no clue about makeup. And you have to drop some pounds. That's a definite. As for your clothes—"

Pandemonium broke out down the hallway. Shouts, barking, and then a series of frantic yelps were followed by the sight of Upton speeding towards us, Julia Roberts, her claws hooked into his curly white coat, grimly riding him like a jockey.

CHAPTER FOUR

"Just how many people are we planning to save?" asked Lonnie, staggering under the weight of a large carton.

Fran, who was superintending the removal of the office supplies to a shed just erected in the backyard and the restocking of the storage room with disaster supplies, snapped, "The Department of Homeland Security has made it very clear that citizens cannot be too prepared. Terrorists could strike at any time."

"You're not answering the question," Lonnie pointed out, depositing the carton where Fran indicated. "You must have enough stuff here for scores of people, and last time I looked, there were only seven of us in the building. You, me, Kylie, Ariana, Bob, Melodie, and Harriet. And Harriet will be on maternity leave any day now."

"Don't forget Julia Roberts," I said.

Lonnie glared at me. "Forget Julia Roberts? Would that I could!"

I felt duty bound to speak up for her. "She was just defending her territory yesterday."

"Defending her territory by lacerating the back of an innocent poodle who was peacefully minding his own business?"

"Jules obviously felt threatened. After all, there were *two* standard poodles, and they're large dogs."

Lonnie put his hands on his pudgy hips. "Since Julia Roberts is yours, I'm expecting you to cover the vet bills."

By all accounts it seemed that Jules had started the whole debacle, so I said, "Fair enough."

"It'll cost you?" Fran observed. "The Feeney woman goes to Dr. Stanley Evers, veterinary surgeon to the stars."

"How do you know that?" Lonnie demanded. "You haven't even got a pet."

"It's none of your business, Lonnie, but if you must know, Quip happened to mention it."

Bob Verritt came around the corner hefting two large cartons, one under each arm. His extremely tall, skinny frame didn't seem substantial enough to handle anything really weighty, but from the thud when he set the cartons down, they were really heavy.

"What in the hell is in these?" he asked.

"Disaster supplies," snarled Fran. "How many times do I have to tell you people?"

"We're stocking up enough to rescue the whole neighborhood?" Bob inquired.

"Of course not," Fran said. "I've taken into account there may be clients in the building when the catastrophe occurs. Besides that, some of us have dear ones we would want to save."

In Fran's case that would be Quip, her husband. The person most dear to me was Ariana. Harriet had Beth. As far as I knew, Bob had no one special, nor did Melodie.

"Would that include poodles?" Lonnie asked. "Pauline won't go anywhere without her poodles."

Fran's pale face was suddenly suffused with red. "No poodles," she ground out, "and certainly no Pauline Feeney. That's final."

I looked at her with surprise. Yesterday in the kitchen, when the star wrangler's name had first come up, Fran hadn't shown any reaction. Now she was positively hostile.

Lonnie glowered at Fran. "Right," he said, throwing up his hands. "If that's your attitude, I've moved my last disaster supply."

Fran shrugged as he marched off with injured dignity in every step. "Touchy, touchy," she said.

"Fair dinkum, Fran, you can't expect Lonnie to be pleased when you refuse to offer aid to his girlfriend."

Fran responded with a contemptuous grunt.

"What have you got against this woman, anyway?" Bob asked.

"She dissed Quip."

"How?"

"I don't want to talk about it." Fran surveyed the storage room, which was already almost half full. "I'm hoping we can fit everything in, otherwise I'll be forced to continue using a corner of your office, Bob."

"That's not an option, Fran!"

Bob was usually so mild-mannered, it was startling to hear him so emphatic. Fran knew when to concede. "OK," she said, "so we'll have to fit it all in here."

"All right, then," said Bob, semi-mollified, "but don't try and pull a fast one on me, Fran."

Fran looked injured. "As if I would."

Bob tossed off one of his braying laughs. "Give you an inch, you take a mile."

"Someone has to take responsibility for safety in these dangerous times," said Fran, affronted. "As the Office Manager, I see it as my duty."

This got another laugh from Bob, but wisely, he didn't comment. Everyone knew that Fran had bestowed the title

Office Manager upon herself, but given her volatile nature, no one was foolish enough to call her on it, even Ariana.

"I'll get the rest of the stuff you have cluttering up my room," Bob announced.

Before collecting my next load of supplies, at present jammed in the janitor's broom cupboard, I gave a sad glance into the storage room. It was next to my bedroom, and I'd had my eye on the space for my own little living room. It would've been simple, I thought, to knock down a couple of walls—provided they weren't load-bearing—and create a much more comfortable area for myself.

A withering look from Fran sent me on my way. I returned with an armful of small boxes, each labeled CAUTION: MEDICAL SUPPLIES in red. "What sort of medical supplies?" I asked, putting the boxes on the shelf Fran's imperious forefinger indicated.

"Various antibiotics for smallpox, anthrax, cholera, and typhoid," said Fran, "and antivirals for bird flu. And of course pre-loaded syringes with morphine for those sustaining major injuries in a quake or explosion."

"Crikey," I said, "is that legal? Having morphine hanging about the place, I mean."

Fran's eyebrows did a dive in an annoyed V. "So you'd prefer to writhe in dreadful pain, would you, Kylie?"

"Well, no, but I wouldn't want to run foul of the authorities either."

"In the middle of a cataclysm, no one's going to be checking the fine print."

Bob suddenly appeared, without cartons, his pleasantly homely face transformed by a dark scowl. "Who ordered a faux Spanish desk for my office?" he demanded. "There are guys at the front from some place called Maximum Spanish trying to deliver it to me. The blasted thing's as big as an aircraft carrier."

"As Office Manager, I ordered the desk?" said Fran. "Is there a problem?"

"Yes, there's a problem. I like my furniture just the way it is."

"We need continuity of decor," Fran declared. "The building itself is Spanish-influenced, and thanks to me the reception desk is now a genuine reproduction Spanish antique. Ariana's office is already Spanish inspired. Over time, I intend to carry this look through to each room."

"Not mine!" exclaimed Bob and I in unison.

Fran never took opposition well. "Neither of you has an ounce of interior decorator vision," she snapped.

"I presume Kendall & Creeling is paying for this furniture?"

"Of course, since it's an office expense."

I didn't lose my temper often, but right now I felt like I was about to blow a gasket. Making an effort to sound icy calm, I said, "Since this grand plan of yours is total news to me, I presume you've cleared it with Ariana. Yes?"

"Not exactly."

That meant no. I glanced at Bob. It wouldn't be good management to haul Fran over the coals in front of him. "Let's talk later," I said to her, "after we finish moving the disaster supplies."

"What about the desk that's already been delivered?" Bob asked. "Those guys were getting mighty impatient."

"Lonnie could take it while Bob gets used to the idea," Fran said.

"Lonnie!" exclaimed Bob and I, again in unison.

The thought of Lonnie coping in the chaos of his room with a gigantic Spanish desk, artificially antiqued, was irresistibly funny. Bob and I dissolved in laughter. Fran didn't smile.

I wiped my eyes, still giggling. "Bob, while you finish moving the stuff for Fran, I'll cancel the order and say there's been a mistake at our end."

Fran opened her mouth, but clearly thought better of it, as she closed it again without a word.

At the front desk, Melodie was charming two stocky delivery men, who were neatly dressed in khaki shorts and shirts. "Kylie, it's real interesting," she said. "Charlie and Pete say they've delivered furniture to tons of stars."

"Scads," said Charlie—I knew which was which because of the names on their shirt pockets—"most are nice, but some are real prima donnas."

"Madonna was a challenge," Pete chimed in. "And Keanu Reeves? Don't ask!"

"I don't doubt it," I said. "Now, about this desk you're delivering…"

"It's out in the courtyard at the moment. Where do you want it?"

"The fact is, we *don't* want it. There's been a mix up with the order. Sorry, but you'll have to take the desk back."

Astonished, Melodie exclaimed, "Take it back! Does Fran know?"

Charlie looked aggrieved. "You mean we've been cooling our heels here all this time, and you don't even want the Grenada?"

"The Grenada?"

"Every desk is named after a Spanish city," said Melodie. "Like, I'm sitting at a Madrid. And I think Fran has a Cordova in mind for you."

Hell's bells! I had to nip this Spanish furniture thing in the bud as soon as poss. "I'm really very sorry," I said to Charlie and Pete, "but we can't accept delivery."

"Throws the sked right out," said Pete lugubriously, "but I don't suppose you care."

"Do I have to sign anything?" I asked.

Charlie handed me an invoice. "Write that you refuse the delivery and give a reason." He added with stern emphasis, "A *good* reason."

When, grumbling, they had gone, Melodie said to me, "Fran's got her heart set on a Spanish furniture makeover. She's going to be real upset you sent the Grenada back. How's she going to explain it to Isabel?"

"And Isabel is…?"

"She and her husband own Maximum Spanish. Like, Fran and Quip are real good friends with Isabel and Spike."

A suspicion began to form in my mind. "Fran isn't getting commission for furniture ordered, is she?"

"Well…"

"So she is?"

Alarm filling her face, Melodie said, "Fran'll kill me. You didn't hear it from me. Please, Kylie."

"I'll try not to blurt it out."

Apparently content with this undertaking, Melodie said cheerfully, "Did I tell you? Larry-my-agent's got me lined up to audition for *Darleen Come Home*. I'm just waiting for him to confirm where and when. I'll be playing Olive, Timmy's long-lost elder sister, come from Australia to visit."

"Bonzer."

Melodie clasped her hands and looked to the ceiling. Starry-eyed, she exclaimed, "Something up there is telling me this is my big chance to break into series television."

I glanced at the ceiling too, but it remained blank. "Some psychic connection has given you the news?"

"*Fate*, Kylie. You do believe in fate, don't you?"

A vision of Cousin Brucie danced in front of my mind. Fate had had a bit of a snigger, making him my rello. "I reckon I do," I said gloomily. "I reckon I do."

* * *

I went off to see Ariana to set her straight on Fran's Spanish phase, but she was just leaving her office as I got there. "Sorry, Kylie, something urgent has come up. I've got to go."

Her face was ashen. Concerned, I said, "Ariana?"

"I can't talk now."

This clearly wasn't the time to ask what was wrong. "No worries," I said. "I'll see you tomorrow."

I looked after Ariana as she left. She had a lovely graceful stride, even when she was rushing, as she was now. I wanted to hurry after her and ask what was it that had upset her. A lover could do that. I felt my shoulders droop. I wasn't even a poor excuse for a lover. As far as Ariana was concerned, I wasn't a lover at all.

Before I could sink further in gloom, I went back to my office and tried Dingo's number again. I left a second voicemail message, a little more urgent than the first.

Soon Mum would be on the phone again asking what steps I'd taken to establish what the problem was with Harry and Gert's son. Merely leaving telephone messages for him wouldn't impress her. Obviously I had to do something more.

No way could I pick a blue with Fran before I told Ariana about the furniture situation, so that particular confrontation was on hold. I got out my Thomas Guide and looked up Dingo O'Rourke's address. It wasn't too far away, and driving there would give me something to concentrate on, other than the dire circumstances of my romantic life. Dingo almost certainly was at work on the set of *Darleen*, but maybe I could find someone to give me some idea of when he might be home.

Dad's red Mustang was a challenge to drive, seeing as it wasn't an automatic, therefore I had to change gears while trying to remember to stay on the right-hand side of the road. In Australia, we drove on the left, like Britain, so I had to say "Keep right!" to myself, especially when making left turns at intersections.

I located Dingo's apartment building on Orange Grove Avenue—a misnamed thoroughfare if ever I saw one—and only had to circle the block a couple of times before I could snaffle a parking spot when someone pulled out.

Dingo's building looked tired, as though it was sick of enduring the summer sun all day while breathing exhaust fumes from the relentless traffic. Sitting on the steps leading to the front entrance was an old lady, her thin silver hair in fat blue rollers. She was wearing a voluminous housecoat and worn pink slippers. She watched my approach with the keenest interest.

"G'day," I said.

"I'm waiting for the mail." She clicked her tongue with irritation. "Postal service they call it, but there's no service to speak off." Squinting up at me, she went on, "They don't care, you see. It's the benefits. Get the benefits whether the mail is delivered or not. Do you know how much a mail carrier makes, with the benefits and all?"

"Fraid not."

"My first husband was a mail carrier." She paused, apparently waiting for me to respond.

"Interesting," I said.

"Interesting? Not Hugo. No one would call him interesting. Now sexy—some called him sexy. Not me, but some did. Divorced him when I found the basement stuffed with undelivered letters. Thousands of them."

"Crikey, that must have been a bit of a jolt."

She nodded acknowledgment. "You've no idea the blow it was. People thought I must have known about the letters, but I never went down into the basement. Creepy place. Anyway, what with all the stares and whispers, I had to leave town. I've never thought the same of mail carriers since." She stared off into the distance, no doubt contemplating Hugo and the undelivered letters.

I sat down beside her on the steps. "I'm looking for Dingo O'Rourke. He has an apartment in this building. You don't happen to know him, do you?"

"Dingo? I know him. Keeps to himself, but we have a few friendly words now and then." She gave me a shrewd glance. "Why are you asking about Dingo? You're not a bill collector, are you?"

"I'm his cousin, a few times removed."

"Another Aussie, eh? Thought you talked funny."

"I've been trying to call him, but had no luck. Left messages, but he doesn't get back to me."

"Twenty-four/seven."

"I beg your pardon?"

She looked around, as if we were under surveillance. Then she leaned over and hissed, "Dingo's staying at the studio, twentyfour/seven. Has to, Darleen being at risk, like she is."

She clutched my arm and got even closer, until her breath was cooling my ear. "Dog-napping."

"Dog-napping?"

She looked uncertain. "Dingo-napping, maybe. Whatever, Dingo's there to make sure it doesn't happen."

CHAPTER FIVE

Maybe it was the threat to Darleen that had made Dingo so unwilling to return my call. Or maybe he was just avoiding me. Mrs. Blake—she told me to call her Phyllis—took my business card and promised to contact me if Dingo turned up at the apartments.

"Not much gets past me," she declared, tucking the card into the pocket of her housecoat. I reckoned that would be pretty well right, since it seemed she spent quite a bit of her time lurking at the entrance to the building.

Phyllis Blake told me Dingo's apartment was on the third floor at the rear, so just in case he did come home somewhere along the line, I scribbled a note on the back of one of my cards and slipped it under his door.

When I came out the front door, the mail had arrived and a large bloke holding a bunch of letters in one huge fist was listening with a resigned expression while Mrs. Blake outlined the shortcomings of the United States Postal Service.

"Have a nice day," he said to me as I squeezed past him on the steps. Mrs. Blake stopped her harangue to wish me a nice day, too.

I'd often wondered why Americans had such an obsession with wishing nice days, but I replied in kind. "Have a totally crash-hot day, yourselves, you two."

They both appeared uncertain at this, so I added, "An excellent day, the sort you like to remember."

She nodded, pleased. The mail bloke muttered something about Mrs. Blake and wishing he could forget. I had a fair idea what he meant.

Driving back to Kendall & Creeling, I mused over how to get to Dingo O'Rourke. It was likely I'd have to go to the studio to catch up with him in person, since voicemails had no effect and he wasn't coming home to his apartment.

Phyllis Blake had assured me that the danger to Darleen was real and ongoing, and that the studio was deeply concerned— she described it as "running around with their asses on fire"— but I didn't recall anything in the news about threats to the show's namesake. Even if the story didn't make the *LA Times* or an evening newscast, surely a show business item like this would have turned up in the trade papers. Melodie scoured *Variety* and *The Hollywood Reporter* every day, so she would know if Darleen's safety was an issue.

Presuming the story was true, it could be that everything was being kept deliberately quiet, although I would have thought it would be great publicity for the show. Maybe there was a lot more to it. Maybe Dingo was mixed up in something nefarious, and that was why he was playing hard to get. For Dingo's sake I'd be cautious, until I knew more.

I turned into Kendall & Creeling's parking area determined to find some way to get onto the set of *Darleen Come Home*. Dad's red Mustang made an untamed, hit-the-open-road kind of statement when I parked it next to my commonplace sedan, which was deliberately bland for tailing suspects. So far I'd only practiced tailing, but any day now I hoped to be pleased I was driving a vehicle so boring it was close to invisible.

Pausing in the courtyard, I admired the little fountain and the other landscaping touches I'd organized. A bolt of resolve ran through me. Over my dead body would a real-estate developer like Norris Blainey replace this with a soulless block of buildings.

I'd already decided not to ask Melodie about any mention of a threat to Darleen in the trades. If there'd been no item about it, just my asking would activate the startlingly efficient receptionists' network, and in mere moments rumors of Darleen's pending napping would be all over town.

Melodie wasn't there. Harriet, hugely pregnant, but looking as healthy and content as one could when so ungainly, was at the front desk.

"Melodie promised me it was a vital audition," she said in explanation. "She pleaded with me to take over the phones."

"And you fell for it?" Melodie had recently promised to attend auditions only in her lunchtimes or after work. Mid-afternoon did not fit the specifications.

Harriet grinned at me. "I got my pound of flesh. She's promised to be available for future baby-sitting duties. Besides, how could I resist when Melodie revealed she'd be auditioning for a part in *Darleen Come Home?* Her big chance, she assured me, to use her excellent Aussie accent."

"Trust me, Melodie's Aussie accent is not much chop."

"Say it isn't so!" said Harriet in mock horror. "Malcolm, Melodie's voice coach, has assured her it's the best he's ever encountered."

The phone rang. Harriet picked up, and I heard her say, "Kylie? She's right here."

I took the receiver, hoping it would be Ariana calling to explain why she'd dashed off earlier, obviously upset. Major disappointment. It wasn't Ariana—it was Cousin Brucie.

"Kylie? This is Bruce. I'm here."

"Great," I said, unable to inject much enthusiasm into my voice. "Did you have a good trip?"

"No complaints."

Maybe Brucie was at the airport, expecting me to pick him up. "Where are you?"

"At a motel. Arrived at LAX early this morning and got a taxi here to the Gateway to the Stars Inn. It's not too far from Kendall & Creeling. Stroke of good luck, eh?"

Fortunately he didn't wait for a reply. "Hang on a mo, Kylie. I've got the address right here somewhere…"

Brucie read me off the phone number and address and I dutifully wrote them down. Summoning up my manners, I said, "Welcome to LA, Brucie."

"Bruce," he said. "I'm dropping Brucie. Too childish. From now on I'm Bruce, like Bruce Willis. More masculine."

"Bruce. I'll try to remember."

"So when can I lob in and meet everyone?"

"You're not jetlagged?" I asked hopefully.

"Naw. That's for people called Brucie. I'm Bruce, remember?"

I blinked. Don't tell me Cousin Brucie actually had a sense of humor! I'd never noticed one before.

It took a bit of persuasion, but I got him to agree not to visit Kendall & Creeling today. I promised to come around later and take Brucie out for an early dinner, since jetlag was sure to hit him mid-evening.

"That was Brucie, Aunt Millie's son?" Harriet asked when I'd hung up.

"The very one."

"I hear he has ambitions to work at Kendall & Creeling."

I wasn't surprised Harriet knew this. "Melodie has spread the word, has she?"

"She says she's looking forward to meeting an Aussie hunk."

That was a laugh. "Cousin Brucie a hunk? Not likely!" I hadn't seen Brucie for a while, but I certainly didn't recollect any hint of hunkdom about him.

A whole set of calls came through at once, so I left Harriet dealing with them and wandered off to the kitchen to make myself a cup of tea and a cheese-and-pickle sandwich to see me through to dinner time. I was pouring the tea when Julia Roberts suddenly appeared. It was almost uncanny, the way she always seemed to know when I was in the kitchen and therefore available to provide nourishment on demand.

"You had breakfast," I pointed out to her. "A substantial breakfast, as I recall. You can't possibly be hungry."

Julia Roberts looked pointedly at the sandwich I'd just made. "Humans are different," I said. "Inferior to cats. We have to eat three times a day." She gave me a blank stare. I sighed. Standing up to Jules was more than I was fit for today. "Prawn and whitefish snacks? Will that be acceptable?"

While she leisurely ate her snacks and I munched on my sandwich, I brooded over Ariana. Why hadn't I just gone ahead and asked her what was wrong when she'd said something urgent had come up? What sort of urgent thing could it be? A range of possible disasters presented themselves: there'd been a rockslide in the Hollywood Hills, and Ariana's beautiful cliff-top house was poised to plummet down the precipitous descent; a colleague from her days as an LAPD cop had been shot and was near death; Ariana had been told she had a serious medical condition; or perhaps Gussie, her gorgeous German Shepherd, had been hurt.

There was one possibility I didn't want to think about, so of course I couldn't *not* think about it. What if it had something to do with Natalie Ives?

Natalie, whom Ariana had loved for so many years—still loved. We'd never met. I'd only seen her in photographs, taken before early-onset Alzheimer's had clouded her mind to the point she'd been admitted to a full-care facility. Ariana saw her every week, even though Natalie only occasionally seemed to have an inkling of who Ariana was.

"It's a triangle, but not a very romantic one." I said to Julia Roberts. She was occupied with washing her whiskers, but paused to give me what I took to be quite a sympathetic look. "In fact, it's pretty much a hopeless situation, Jules."

I leaned over to stroke her, not for her comfort, but to soothe myself. Her sleek fur whispered under my palm as she arched her back. She whipped around in a graceful circle and came back for another caress. "Beerrow," she said, a mark of warm approval.

For some reason her appreciation upset me. If I sat here any longer, I'd dissolve into a puddle of self-pity. I gave her a final stroke and took myself along to Lonnie's office. I knocked on his door and adroitly whisked through a narrow opening before Julia Roberts, who'd followed closely, could join us.

"That psychopathic cat's lurking out there, isn't she?" said Lonnie glumly.

"Fair dinkum, Lonnie, I've told you a thousand times she's teasing you. If you could bring yourself to totally ignore Jules, she'd start to lose interest fast."

"You don't understand. She's possessed of an evil spirit."

"You're joking, right?"

He nodded reluctantly. "I suppose...but she's a devil cat." He brushed his hands together in a that's-that gesture. "I've wasted enough time on Julia Roberts. You've heard my last word on the subject."

I hid a smile. There'd never be a last word. He was as obsessed with Julia Roberts as Julia Roberts was obsessed with him.

Lonnie had moved the garden gnome he'd recently acquired from the floor by his chair to a position on his crowded computer desk. I gave the grotesque little figure the once-over. Although it had the characteristics of a standard gnome—garish red and green clothing, a long beard, and a ferocious scowl—it wasn't a roughly cast, mass-produced statue, but clearly handmade.

"Pauline Feeney gave you this, didn't she?" I said in a burst of inspiration.

Lonnie pinked up immediately. "Maybe."

"Lonnie?"

"Oh, all right. Yes, it was Pauline's gift to me."

"It's beautifully made. Something quite out of the ordinary."

Chuffed by my praise, Lonnie said, "Pauline's something quite out of the ordinary, too."

"She certainly seems to be."

"Best thing that ever happened to me." Lonnie's smile faded. He was obviously sorry that he'd let his guard down, so he went on briskly, "Did you want something in particular, or is this a social call?"

I knew it was perfectly safe to raise the topic of Darleen's possible abduction with Lonnie, as long as I said it was confidential. "I'd rather you didn't mention this anywhere," I said. Lonnie mimed zipping his lips, so I continued, "I've heard a rumor there's some plot to abduct Darleen the dingo, the star of *Darleen Come Home*, for ransom. Have you heard anything?"

Lonnie's expression showed his keen interest. "Not a word, but it could be true. The show's the biggest hit Bellina Studios have had since their slate of reality programs tanked. Darleen would be well worth snatching, even though she's not the only dingo they've got."

This was news to me. "There's more than one Darleen?"

"There's the main Darleen, but there'll be one or two backups. You don't want shooting to grind to a halt because the star animal is sick, or has been hurt. It's a time-honored tradition. You don't think there was only one Lassie, do you? Or Rin Tin Tin, or Mr. Ed—"

"Stop," I said. "I get the idea."

"I'll ask around, discreetly of course. Bellina Studios run a tight ship, but there's always someone who'll leak any sensational news."

Knowing how Lonnie spent a good part of his time online, I was confident if there was any chatter about an extortion scheme involving Darleen, Lonnie would find it.

I told him about Dingo O'Rourke and how, because of distant family ties, I'd been compelled to investigate what was up with him. "I can't get Dingo to answer my calls, so I reckon I need to get onto the television set and front up to him face-to-face. The problem is, I don't know how to go about it."

"Studio security."

"Security is what's keeping me out."

"Security's what will get you in. Talk to Ariana. She's sure to have a contact through the LAPD. Many ex-cops end up in security."

I'd love to talk to Ariana, but not necessarily about security at Bellina Studios. I left Lonnie enthusiastically starting his search for information on possible dingo-napping and went back to my office. I tried Ariana's cell, but only got voicemail. I didn't leave a message. Then I called her house. The answering machine cut in after three rings.

Feeling angry and apprehensive and helpless all at once, I called her cell again and left a message: "Ariana, it's me, Kylie. Please call me when you get a chance." I'd intended to say I was concerned about her, to ask if there was anything I could do, but I chickened at the last moment. It was probably a good thing I did, I decided. Ariana was so intensely private that she'd recoil if I got too pushy.

I was so het up about everything that I couldn't sit still. I ran into Fran outside the storage room, now officially the disaster supplies room. She was in the process of affixing a sign to the door. It read:

DESIGNATED DISASTER SUPPLIES. FOR USE ONLY IN A GENUINE CATASTROPHE. ANY OTHER USE STRICTLY PROHIBITED. IF IN ANY DOUBT, CONTACT OFFICE MANAGER FOR A LIST OF ACCEPTABLE CALAMITIES.

"Strewth!" I said. "Acceptable calamities? Wouldn't it be obvious even to blind Freddy when it was a total disaster?"

Fran shot me a chilly look. "It might be obvious to blind Freddy, whoever he is, that a genuine catastrophe has occurred, but I'm more concerned with the likes of Lonnie. He's got no common sense, and is liable to raid the supplies just for some piddling accident."

I was about to ask what the harm was if he did use some of the stuff in the event of an accident, when Fran said in a challenging tone, "Melodie tells me you're not keen on the Cordova. I particularly chose that model for you. However, if you'd prefer another desk, the Cadiz is very attractive. I can supply an illustrated catalog."

That did it! To hell with waiting to consult with Ariana! "Fran, I want you in my office, now," I said. "We have to discuss this whole matter of the faux Spanish furniture."

For a moment, Fran looked uncertain, then her diminutive form seemed to swell a little as her Amazonian persona reasserted itself. "I can give you a few minutes," she said with the air of one granting a favor.

"You can give me as long as it takes."

It would have been nice if Fran had meekly followed me to my office. Nice, but unrealistic. Instead she strode militantly ahead of me, arms swinging.

As we reached my door, I said, "I'm surprised you're not whistling a happy tune."

"What?"

I sang her a few bars from *The King and I.* Fran rolled her eyes, snarled, "Oh, *please!*" and then marched into my office, every line of her body suggesting she wasn't afraid.

To bolster my authority—not that it needed much bolstering at this point, as my rage was taking care of that—I sat down at my desk and pointed to the visitor's chair on the other side. "Sit."

Fran plunked herself in the chair and glared at me defiantly. "Well?"

Making a real effort to be imperturbable, I said, "Your friends, Isabel and Spike, own Maximum Spanish."

I thought she'd ask how I knew this, but all she said was, "So?"

"Without clearing it with me or with Ariana, you decided to order furniture for Kendall & Creeling from your friends' business."

"I *am* the Office Manager."

"You don't have the authority to spend that kind of money without checking first."

Fran folded her arms under her impressive breastworks. "Ariana would have said yes, I know she would."

"You don't know that. And it's not only Ariana's decision. It's mine, too."

Fran shrugged. "Sorry," she drawled.

"But there's something that disturbs me even more."

"Hmmm?" Fran's expression was one of complete boredom.

"Perhaps I'm just a little Aussie sheila, but from where I come from, secretly taking commission for goods—in this case furniture—ordered on behalf of your employer is unconscionable."

Fran's pale face flushed. "I…" She seemed to shrink in the chair. "We need the money. We've got problems."

"What do you mean?"

"It's Quip. He's writing a novel. It's taking up every moment of his time."

I knew that Quip, even though he'd never had a movie produced, still managed to make a living consulting as a script doctor. And there was the stage play he'd written and directed. When I mentioned this, Fran gave a bitter laugh.

"The play ran at a loss. In fact, we borrowed to pay for the theater, and the box office nowhere near covered our costs."

Fran looked so embarrassed to be telling me this, I felt a pang of pity. "Maybe Quip's novel will be a big success. What's it about?"

"At first Quip was going to write about the dark underbelly of Hollywood. How the entertainment industry grinds you up and spits you out."

Even an outsider like me thought this sounded awfully familiar. "It's a theme that's been covered lots of times before, hasn't it?"

"That's what I told him—Hollywood underbelly stories are a dime a dozen." Fran's expression lightened and a smile appeared on her lips. "Quip's so talented. He came up with a new concept almost immediately."

"A coming-of-age novel, perhaps?" I inquired.

Fran's smile disappeared. "Are you trying to be funny? Everyone knows coming-of-age novels are a dime a dozen too."

"Crikey, Fran. Spit it out. What's he writing?"

"Quip was going to base his novel on the career and times of Donald Trump, but then he had a revelation, and switched to Norris Blainey. It's called *I, Developer.*"

"The Norris Blainey who's aiming to tear down this building and ruin the neighborhood?"

"The very one. The novel's a searing expose of Blainey's dirty dealings and ruthless tactics, but in Quip's novel he's called Morris Rainey."

"I've got to give it to Quip," I said. "Not in a million years will Norris Blainey tumble to the fact it's him."

"Of course everyone will know it's Blainey," said Fran with ill-disguised impatience. "That's the point."

"And he won't sue for defamation?"

"Blainey's a public figure. Unless Quip makes up outrageous lies that destroy what little reputation the man still has, Blainey can't sue him."

It sounded a bit dicey to me—I'd got the impression Norris Blainey would be an enemy you'd rather not have—but I said stoutly, "I'm sure *I, Developer* will be a rip-snorter of a novel."

"I know it will be. Quip's a *wonderful* writer."

I'd always admired—and envied—Fran's total belief in Quip and his talents. She loved and supported him unreservedly. I was musing on how bonzer it would be if Ariana felt this way about me, when I became aware that Fran had an expression on her face I had never seen before. It threw me for a moment, then I realized it was her version of entreaty.

"Kylie, please don't tell anyone about our money problems." She paused, then with a struggle, forced out the words, "I'm begging you."

"You don't have to beg me. Does Ariana know about this? I'll have to tell her."

Fran shook her head. "No one knows."

"Not even your mother?" Ariana's sister was a successful artist. I found Janette's paintings rather disturbing, but they sold well, so I presumed she was in a position to help out.

"Mom doesn't know. Quip's proud. He doesn't want to ask for charity."

"He'd rather you sneaked commission on the sly?"

Another new expression crossed Fran's face. Could it be mortification? I thought it was.

"Quip doesn't know anything about the commission," she said. "Isabel and Spike agreed to keep it secret."

I found this new, unsettled Fran disconcerting. I wanted the old, acerbic, warrior-princess Fran back. "I'd be surprised if you wanted my advice, but I'll give it anyway. Discuss all this with Ariana."

This got a grudging nod from Fran. She got to her feet. "Is our little talk over?" she asked, with a flash of her usual caustic self.

"If you agree to no more Spanish furniture."

She nodded reluctantly. "OK."

Lonnie came shooting through the door as Fran was leaving. "Watch it!" she snarled.

He waited until she'd gone, then said to me. "The Collie Coalition."

"What's that?"

"The shadowy group threatening to snatch Darleen. They're outraged that a dingo is playing the role that Lassie the collie made famous."

I grinned. "The Collie Coalition? What a joke."

Lonnie wasn't laughing. "Homeland Security have them pegged as a terrorist group," he said.

CHAPTER SIX

The next morning I was up with the birds, keen to get the Dingo situation sorted out. Ariana had called me last evening while I'd been getting ready for my dinner date with Brucie. Her voice had been subdued, her usual crisp tones blurred with fatigue. "I'll be in the office tomorrow afternoon," she said before I could ask any leading questions. "In the meantime, is there anything I should know about?"

"Nothing that can't wait. Oh, except for one thing." I'd told her how I needed to get into Bellina Studios to see the elusive Dingo O'Rourke. "Lonnie says it's possible you might know an ex-cop working in the studio security unit."

"I can do better than that. The present head of security is Eppie Longworth. She and I worked together in the LAPD and we've kept in touch. I'll call her and get back to you."

I hadn't expected Ariana to do anything about it until the next day, so I'd been surprised when fifteen minutes later she was on the line again. "Your name will be on the entry list at the gate. Eppie will be expecting you. She's on duty from eight tomorrow morning."

"Ariana?"

I'd heard her sigh. "Don't ask, Kylie. Tomorrow, OK?"

The sigh stung. Feeling defensive, I'd said, "I'm not trying to be a pest. I'm worried about you."

"Don't be."

Fair dinkum, loving someone could be a real downer at times!

Meeting Brucie for dinner was somewhat of an anti-climax, as I was distracted because of my conversation with Ariana, and Brucie, despite his protestations, had been hit hard by jetlag and could barely keep his eyes open. I picked him up at the seriously seedy Gateway to the Stars Inn and took him to a nearby Italian restaurant.

He'd changed since I'd last seen him, but I couldn't immediately put my finger on how. For one thing, I hadn't remembered Brucie as being particularly good-looking; however, a dispassionate assessment of his physical self—dark curly hair; smooth coffee skin like his mother; a lean, taut body—added up to something quite close to handsome.

Handsome or not, as far as I was concerned, Brucie's character had always been the problem, although my mum always said it was a two-way street, with the clash of our personalities fueling the fire.

Over dinner Brucie—I had to fight to call him Bruce—chatted in a desultory way about family news. Astonishingly, we didn't get into an argument, which was a first for us. In the past we'd be at daggers drawn within minutes of running into each other.

He asked me about Dingo O'Rourke, and I told him I was hoping to get onto the *Darleen Come Home* soundstage the next morning. Naturally, Brucie wanted to come too, which caused our first disagreement of the evening.

I finally conceded that if he turned up at Kendall & Creeling tomorrow afternoon he could meet everyone, plus

I would undertake to fill him in on my hoped-for face-to-face with Dingo at Bellina Studios.

* * *

While I was having my breakfast of porridge, toast, and tea, Melodie came bouncing into the kitchen. "I know I'm early," she announced to my raised eyebrows. She added virtuously, "Like, I'm making up time, since I had a can't-miss audition yesterday afternoon."

"That's ambiguous," I observed. "Is it a can't-miss audition because it's important? Or is it a can't-miss audition meaning you've aced it and you can't miss out on the role?"

Melodie frowned at me. "You can be real puzzling at times, Kylie." Her face cleared as she went on, "But since you ask, Larry-my-agent says I'm a sure thing for Olive."

Abruptly, her expression changed to one of emotional overload and she began to wring her hands. "Oh, Timmy," she cried with an excruciating nasal accent, "is that really you? Strike me lucky! Leaping lizards, it's my fair dinkum baby brother! Whoops-a-daisy! By gum, to think we've been torn asunder all these yonks, with me Down Under and you here, in Texas, and never a cooee between us. And Darleen, how chuffed I am that you've been dinky-di faithful to Timmy."

"Hell's bells, is that a good example of the show's dialogue? Sounds crook to me."

The frown was back on Melodie's face. "What do you mean, crook?"

"It's no good. In fact, it's laughably bad."

"You're in no position to judge these things, Kylie. Screen dialogue is an artistic rendition of conversation. Like, it's not *real*."

"It certainly isn't. No Aussie wrote that rubbish."

My scathing tone seriously irked Melodie. "You being a total outsider and all, I don't suppose you've even heard of the writer/director of *Darleen Come Home*, Earl Garfield. He's had so many successful series, he's like, a *god* in this town. Quip says he's a scriptwriter's scriptwriter. The best."

I knew who Earl Garfield was, having done some online research into the show yesterday. Years ago Garfield had been the TV industry's boy wonder. Now I guessed he'd be the industry's middle-aged wonder. "This Garfield bloke writes every script, does he?"

"He wouldn't have time to do that *and* direct," said Melodie with the tone of one talking to someone terminally dim, "so he employs a team of writers. But he'd read every word. There's nothing gets by him. He's famous for controlling every facet of his show."

"Crikey, he's not controlling the quality of the scripts if what I just heard is any indication."

A dreamy look appeared on Melodie's face. "It was one of my best auditions, Kylie. I shone! Although it's only for two episodes at the moment, I'm hoping once they see me in action, the character will be written into further episodes. Larry-my-agent told me the casting director was just bowled over by my Olive, so I expect to be meeting Earl Garfield soon. Of course, he has the final word on the cast."

She mused on this happy event for a moment, then said, "I mean, not just *anybody* meets him. Garfield's a famous recluse, who won't give interviews or socialize. Like Bette Davis."

"I think you mean Greta Garbo."

Melodie flapped a hand. "Whatever."

"There's a fair chance I'll be seeing Mr. Garfield this morning."

That got Melodie's wide-eyed attention. "You're visiting your dingo wrangling relative today? On the set of *Darleen Come Home?*"

"I'll give it a burl."

She wrinkled her nose at me. "Like it'd be nice if you spoke plain English for a change."

"I said I'm going to attempt to see Dingo."

"Don't move." Melodie rushed off, her high heels beating a rhythm down the hall. A couple of moments she was back, a large photo in her hand. "It's my best headshot," she said, shoving it at me. "If you could just get Timmy to sign it, or failing that, anyone else in the cast, that would be awesome!"

The first time I'd been asked to do this I'd been working undercover at a celebrity doctor's offices. At the time I'd thought it very odd to ask for a star's autograph on someone else's photograph. Now I knew nothing was too strange for the entertainment industry.

"I'll try," I said, "but no guarantees."

Melodie gave me a quick hug. "You're the best, Kylie. Of course, the chances are I'll soon be on the set myself as Olive, Timmy's sister. Still, I never like to miss an opportunity, just in case."

"Too true," I said, "some sheila might snatch the part from you."

Melodie smiled complacently. "Larry-my-agent says I'm the closest he's ever seen to a sure thing."

* * *

I drove my unexciting, anonymous wheels to Bellina Studios. The address was in a semi-industrial part of Los Angeles and I got lost a couple of times while avoiding huge trucks that seemed determined to squash my car like a tin can.

Finally I located my destination. Bellina Studios covered a considerable area, and comprised a collection of industrial buildings, all slightly shabby but serviceable. Huge billboards advertised the shows made there. *Darlene Come Home* held pride of place, with the Hardestie family grouped together, their smiles impossibly warm, while Darleen—more sleek than any dingo I'd seen in the wild—sat beside them staring nobly into the distance.

I turned through the entrance gates and obediently rolled to a stop at a Stop Here sign. The truculent guard in a pale gray uniform stepped out of the booth and eyeballed me. "Name?"

"Kylie Kendall." His first name appeared on his chest, so I said, "G'day, Desmond."

"Trunk."

"I beg your pardon?"

"Trunk." When I stared at him, puzzled, he said, each word distinct, "Open your trunk."

Now it was clear to me what Desmond meant. "Oh, you mean the *boot*."

He didn't reply, but marched to the back of my car. I pressed the release. After a moment he slammed down the lid. He came back to me, squinted at his list, ticked off my name, handed me a clip-on that proclaimed AUTHORIZED VISITOR, and directed me to the furthest corner of the parking lot.

Before I set off, he pointed to nearby sliding glass doors. "Park and lock your vehicle, then come back here and go through those doors to security, where you'll collect your host."

"I don't just get a map of the place with an X marking the spot?" I asked with a grin.

"All visitors have to be accompanied by designated hosts while on the studio grounds," he said. He added, after a meaningful pause, "I'll be watching you."

He wasn't kidding. From the time I got out of the car and headed back across the lot, he had binoculars trained on me. I gave him a cheerful wave before I disappeared inside. He didn't wave back.

I went up to the reception desk and gave my name to a blond woman who was pretty much a clone of Melodie, only not so good-looking. Eppie Longworth, Ariana's erstwhile colleague, came out of her office to greet me. She was wearing the same pale gray uniform as the guard at the gate, but hers sported a badge reading HEAD OF SECURITY. She was medium height, with a stocky build and a no-nonsense air. She had a crash-hot smile, which transformed her rather plain face into something close to beautiful.

"Call me Eppie," she said, shaking my hand. "Ariana tells me you're keen to become a licensed private investigator."

"I'm giving it a go."

"Pity you've never been in law enforcement. As an amateur, you've got quite a few more supervised hours to accumulate than an ex-cop."

"Too true," I said. "Thousands." I added quickly, in case she thought I was a no-hoper, "But I'm going to stick it out, no matter what."

She laughed. "Ariana said as much."

It gave me a ridiculous little thrill to think Ariana had mentioned something personal about me. I only just stopped myself from looking like a total galah by asking, "What else did she say about me?"

Eppie took me through to the back of the building where dozens of electric carts were lined up. Several people were lounging about, chatting. I took it they were the hosts the guard at the gate had mentioned.

"I'll take you to the *Darleen* soundstage myself," said Eppie, sliding into the driving seat of the nearest cart. I got in beside her.

As we jolted along a cobblestone street—I vaguely recognized the facades around us as belonging to some series I'd seen on television—Eppie said, "I gather Doug O'Rourke is a relative of yours?"

"Distant. Dingo's a cousin removed a few times."

"This isn't a social call?"

"Not really." I told her how Harry and Gert O'Rourke had become worried when he'd become uncharacteristically uncommunicative. "I'm here to say g'day and find out if anything's wrong with him."

She flicked a quick look at me, then said, "O'Rourke had a full background check before he was employed by Bellina. Passed with flying colors."

This was mildly surprising, as Dingo had always been a bit of a wild bloke, though he'd never been in the slammer.

Being as Eppie was head of security, and should know what was going on, I said, "Have you heard of the Collie Coalition?"

"I don't believe so," she said, her tone dismissive.

"There's a rumor going around that Darleen the dingo's likely to be taken for ransom."

Eppie's face went blank. "There are always rumors circulating in television. It comes with the territory."

"So there's no truth in this particular one?"

"I guarantee Darleen isn't going anywhere," she said firmly.

This wasn't really an answer to my question, but before I could probe further, Eppie brought the electric cart to a stop outside a large, windowless building.

"This is it, Kylie. I'll take you in and introduce you, then I've got work to do. Tell them to call me when you're ready to leave."

Inside it was organized chaos. The place was crammed with equipment and sets and cameras and lights. Cables ran everywhere on the floor. People were rushing to and fro, seemingly intent on urgent tasks, while others lounged around talking.

Eppie cut a path through to an inoffensive-looking bloke who was standing by himself earnestly checking through items on a clipboard. "Freddie, this is Kylie Kendall. She's here to see Dingo O'Rourke."

He didn't seem at all put out to be interrupted in this way. "Right. Follow me."

I said goodbye to Eppie, then hurried to keep up with Freddie, who moved with deceptive speed. He took me through a dizzying array of sets then down a long hallway to a green door bearing the stern commandment to keep it closed at all times. "Through here."

Behind it was a large room fitted with three spacious mesh runs. One of them, I guessed, held the famous Darleen.

Dingo was slumped in a chair, smoking. He looked up as we entered, his face far from welcoming. "What do you want?"

"Dingo," I said. "G'day."

Freddie said, "I'll leave you to it," and disappeared.

"Jesus, Kylie, what are you doing here?"

"Just dropping in to say hello."

Dingo dropped the butt of his cigarette on the floor and ground it out under the heel of his boot. "It's not a good time."

He was thinner and more drawn than I remembered. His sandy hair was lank and lifeless. Even his mustache drooped listlessly. He still had a hard, muscled body, but his usually tanned face was pale and there was a tremor in his hands.

"Why didn't you answer my calls?" I asked.

"Christ, can't you leave me alone?"

"This isn't my idea, Dingo. I'm here as a favor to your mum and dad."

His face twisted. "Tell them I'm fine."

"You don't look fine to me."

"I haven't got time for this."

He looked relieved when the door opened and a girl stuck her head through. "Darleen's up in fifteen."

"I can't talk now. Later perhaps, Kylie. I'll call you."

We both knew he wouldn't.

I found my way back to the activity by heading towards the noise. I was looking for Freddie to call Eppie Longworth to come and get me, when a balding bloke with a ponytail grabbed me.

"You're late! Here, take this." He took my arm and guided me over to one of the sets. Shoving pages of script into my hand, he said, "Take it from the top."

"There's been some mistake—"

"No mistake. That's the scene I want." He turned away to bellow, "Giles? Where the hell are you? Get some light on this girl."

Abruptly, blinding lights came on. I blinked through the glare at the pages I was holding, recognizing the first words. It was the appallingly written passage Melodie had delivered in the kitchen this morning.

Someone yelled, "Quiet on the set!" Silence immediately fell.

"And action!" snapped the ponytailed bloke, who had to be Earl Garfield.

Right. I'd give him action. I'd show him how it should have been written. I'd ham it up and have some fun.

"Timmy?" I cried, hoping my expression conveyed a combo of wonder and desperate hope. "Fair dinkum, is that really you? My baby brother?" I took a deep breath to prolong a dramatic pause, then went on, "You little bobby-dazzler! At last, after all these years, with me in Oz and you here, in Texas, and never a word between us. Ripper!" I dropped my gaze to an imaginary dingo by his side. "And good onya, Darleen, for being true blue."

"Cut!" Garfield strode into the light. "Your accent needs some work, but you'll do. The part's yours."

"But—"

"Giles will look after the details." He raised his voice to yell, "Giles, where the hell are you?"

"Mr. Garfield—"

"Don't bother me"—he broke off to peer at me intently— "Name?"

"Kylie, Kylie Kendall."

"Don't bother me with piddling trivia, Kylie Kendall. Your agent will handle negotiations."

"I don't have—"

"Giles! Get your ass over here!" He turned back to glare at me. "And be on time in future."

"What just happened?" I said to Giles.

"You got the part of Olive. Congratulations. You're a TV star."

CHAPTER SEVEN

I got back to Kendall & Creeling feeling rather like a stunned mullet. I skipped past Melodie at the front desk with a pang of guilt, wondering how to break the news that I was about to play Olive, not her. I found Ariana wasn't in yet, and I required expert advice, fast.

"Bob," I said, closing Bob Verritt's office door behind me, "I need help. Urgently."

He looked up from the papers he'd been reading. "What have you done now?"

"Now?" I said, indignant. "It's not like I make a habit of getting myself into trouble."

That made Bob laugh immoderately. "Kylie, it's your modus operandi."

I smiled reluctantly. Unfortunately, there was some truth in the charge.

Still grinning, Bob leaned his skinny frame back in his chair. "So what's the problem?"

"I've sort of become an actor, by accident."

I told Bob the sequence of events that had led to my being offered the role of Olive. He indulged in more unrestrained laughter.

"Can't tell you how pleased I am that I amuse you so much," I said, rather miffed at his lighthearted attitude.

Making a real effort to be serious, Bob said, "So why didn't you tell Garfield it was a case of mistaken identity?"

"I was going to, and then it hit me that this would be a perfect way to spend some time near Dingo O'Rourke and find out what's going on with him. Dingo made it pretty clear he's not intending to see me again, but he won't have any choice if I'm in the cast. And don't worry about me being out of the office. Olive's only scheduled for two episodes, so it won't be a longterm thing."

Bob's grin broke out again. "You could make a big splash in the part. If that happens, your character will join the permanent cast."

"There's Buckley's chance of that. What I know about acting could be written on the head of a pin, and in block letters. That's why I need your advice."

"Were you asked if you had an agent?"

"I almost said Melodie's Larry-my-agent represented me, but then I thought that might not be wise."

"Good grief," said Bob, the smile wiped off his face. "Melodie! She's not going to be happy."

This struck me as quite an understatement. "Melodie's going to be mad as a cut snake. She'd been telling everybody how she aced her audition for Olive and that she's a sure thing for the part."

"I'd keep out of dark alleys, if I were you."

There was silence while we both contemplated Melodie's likely reaction. Hostile was probably the best I could hope for under the circumstances. Completely berko was more likely.

"Bob, I'm a babe in the woods about this acting stuff," I said, "and I can hardly ask Melodie's advice."

"Let's give this some serious thought. OK, first you need an agent or an entertainment lawyer to represent you and negotiate your contract. Since you've already got the job, I'm thinking a lawyer's the way to go. Ask Harriet—she'll recommend someone first-class. And you need to join SAG or AFTRA, whichever has jurisdiction over *Darleen Come Home*." He added helpfully, "That's the Screen Actors Guild and the American Federation of Television and Radio Artists."

I sighed. "This acting lark's more complicated than I bargained for."

"Just wait until you get a taste of Earl Garfield as autocratic director," said Bob with a wry smile. "He's been known to make grown men cry."

* * *

Harriet was as amused as Bob had been, but she did manage to stifle her giggles long enough to call an entertainment lawyer friend, and set up an appointment for later that afternoon. Swearing her to silence, as I had yet to tell Melodie the bad news, I went looking for Julia Roberts. At times like this Jules was an excellent sounding board. I'd use her to trial a few different ways to introduce the inconvenient fact that I'd inadvertently stolen the part Melodie coveted.

I couldn't locate Jules, and as she had any number of hidey holes where she could be lurking, I gave up the idea of using her as a test audience. I knew I had no excuse to put off the awful moment any longer. My mother's oft-repeated advice echoed in my ears: "Strike while the iron is hot. She who hesitates is lost. Bite the bullet…"

Mum. Of course she'd be anxious to hear what was going on with Dingo. I persuaded myself I'd give her a quick call and catch her early before things got hectic at The Wombat's Retreat. Then I'd dash Melodie's hopes.

Jack O'Connell, my mum's fiancé, answered the phone. "Jeez, Kylie, you've rung at a bad time. We've got a bloody emergency, no two ways about it."

He put the phone down before I could ask what sort of emergency it was. After a long delay, Mum came on the line. "Can't talk, darl. The kitchen staff's just walked off the job. There's no one to cook breakfast, and wouldn't you know it, we've got a full complement of guests. I've got everyone pitching in, including Millie."

"What upset the kitchen staff?"

"Jack upset them, that's who. Rubbing them up the wrong way, telling them how to do their jobs..."

I could see where this was heading. "I'll let you go, Mum, and call later, when—"

"I need you here at the Wombat, Kylie. I can't run the place on my own, and Jack's no help, as you can see. So when are you coming home?"

I was saved from answering by a hubbub at the other end of the line. "Gotta go, love. Jack says they're coming to blows in the kitchen."

Right. Now I'd speak with Melodie. Before I was out my office door, the phone on my desk rang.

"Is that you, Kylie? The nice young woman I met yesterday?"

"Mrs. Blake?"

"Phyllis, please." She dropped her voice to a hoarse whisper. "Something odd. I thought you should know."

When silence indicated a prompt was needed, I said, "Know what, Phyllis?"

"This morning I just happened to be getting a bit of air out the front of our building, when these two men turned up. Asking questions about Dingo. Shifty-eyed. Very suspicious."

"Do you have any idea who they were?"

"Naturally, as a matter of course I asked for ID," said Phyllis, sounding a little hurt that I hadn't realized this. "I've watched enough shows on television to know you ask for ID. So I did. 'Show me some ID,' I said."

"And did they?"

"That panicked them a bit." Phyllis had a note of satisfaction in her voice. "Looked at each other, then the one who seemed to be the leader told me that they were just friends of Douglas O'Rourke's. I knew immediately they were up to no good. I said, 'You're no friends of his if you're calling him Douglas. He's Dingo to his friends. So who are you?' And they said not to worry, and left. I thought it best to follow them. You've got to be proactive about crime these days."

I had a vision of Mrs. Blake in her slippers and housecoat trotting along behind these two slippery-looking blokes. "Stone the crows, Phyllis, that sounds like a dangerous thing to do."

"Not at all. I always carry my personal alarm in my pocket. A touch of a finger and an ear-splitting noise gets everyone's attention. I had my hand on it the whole time. One of them looked over his shoulder and saw me, then the two of them rushed to get into a big black limo."

"You didn't get the number, did you?"

Phyllis sighed. "Sorry, dearie, no. My eyes aren't as good as they used to be."

I grabbed a pen. "Could you describe them to me?"

This took some time, as Phyllis was nothing if not thorough. As I jotted the last detail down, she said, "At first I thought they might be mafia, you know, like in the movies. But these two weren't good enough for that. And they weren't bill collectors. Bill collectors come straight out with it and don't beat around the bush like these bozos."

I wasn't quite sure what a bozo was, but it didn't sound flattering. "Maybe you should call the cops if you see these two blokes again."

"The cops?" said Phyllis with scorn. "I can look after myself. Tell you what, if they turn up again, I'll call you."

I got her to promise to be careful, and said goodbye. Excuses over. I stiffened my upper lip and headed for the front desk. Melodie had company.

"G'day, Kylie," said Cousin Brucie. "You never told me someone as beaut-looking as Melodie worked here. If I'd known, I'd have lobbed in even sooner." He gave her a big smile. "I can see it's true what they say about California girls."

Melodie beamed. To me she said, "And you never told me your cousin Bruce was so handsome."

"Must have slipped my mind."

Looking at them, I had to admit they made an attractive couple. Melodie obviously agreed, because she said, "I've just been telling Bruce I'd love to show him around some of our night spots."

"Terrif idea," I said with enthusiasm. Anything to get Brucie off my hands. I cleared my throat. "Melodie, I need to talk to you about something, in private."

Inconveniently, someone chose this moment to call Kendall & Creeling. While Melodie was answering the phone, Brucie said to me, "Well? What's the good oil? Did you see Dingo?"

"Just for a few minutes."

"And…?"

"And nothing, Brucie, yet."

"Bruce," he said, grimacing. "Bruce."

"Oh, sorry. I keep forgetting. Bruce it is."

I became aware that Melodie was staring at me. She said into the receiver, "Say it again, Tiff."

Tiffany apparently said it again, because Melodie's face went dead white and her eyes narrowed to slits. "You're sure?" she said.

Apparently Tiff was sure. Melodie put down the receiver with exaggerated care, got slowly to her feet, fixing me with a look that threatened severe bodily harm.

"Corblimey," said Brucie, seeing the California girl he'd just admired transformed into something dangerously feral.

With horror I realized I'd dallied too long. The receptionists' network had beaten me to it. "Let me explain," I said to Melodie.

"How could you, Kylie? You knew I was counting on Olive. You *knew!*"

"The whole thing was an accident, honestly, Melodie."

"Olive was mine!" A tremor ran through her. "And you can't even act."

"It was my Aussie accent," I said. "That's the only possible explanation."

Melodie pointed at me with a dramatic gesture. "You... you... Benedict Arnold!"

"Who's Benedict Arnold?" Brucie asked.

Melodie flashed a corrosive glance in his direction. "A traitor," she hissed, "like Kylie."

"Hey, fair crack of the whip," Brucie protested. "Kylie's got lots of faults, but being a traitor isn't one of them."

"Thanks for the ringing endorsement," I said.

To my consternation, Melodie put her face in her hands and began to cry. "My big chance ruined," she wailed.

A furious Melodie I could cope with, but a weeping Melodie made me feel lower than a snake's belly. "I'm sorry—"

"Sorry? You're *sorry?*" Melodie pushed past me and tottered off down the hall, her shoulders heaving with heavy sobs.

"Holy mackerel!" said Brucie.

I was about to go after her when the phone rang. It was a call for Lonnie. As I put that through to him, another call came in, this time for Harriet. I rang her line, and before I put the call through I said, "Harriet, this is a true emergency. Can you take over the front desk when you're finished with this call?" Harriet, agreeable as always, said she would.

Brucie had settled himself on the corner of the desk. "What in the hell did you do?" he asked with a grin. "And who's this Olive sheila?"

"Where to begin?" I said.

Fran appeared, scowling. "What's wrong with Melodie? She just ran past me, sobbing."

"Let's put it this way, Fran, it's a bit complicated."

"I did catch a few words. Something about someone two-faced snatching the role of a lifetime from her."

"That would be me," I said.

* * *

I left early for my appointment with the entertainment lawyer Harriet had lined up, just to get out of the office. Brucie was entertaining Fran with stories about his mother. Fran had met Aunt Millie, and heartily approved of her bleak view of life, as it matched Fran's own.

Melodie had cried herself out and had returned to her post at the front desk in ice-princess mode. She had been cruelly wronged, and frigid dignity would be her response.

"We'll talk later," I said to her as I opened the front door. Melodie's glance was frosty. "There's absolutely nothing left to say, so please don't bother."

I could hardly blame Melodie for her angst. On the way to my car I brooded over whether I should have taken the role or not, but decided there was no guarantee Melodie would have got it anyway. In fact, since Earl Garfield was still auditioning for Olive when he grabbed me by mistake, the odds were Melodie had already dipped out.

For a moment I considered sharing this insight with Melodie. Perhaps not.

I was just about to get into my Toyota sedan when Lonnie, hot and bothered, came hurrying over. "Kylie, before you go…"

"What's up? Is there some prob?"

"I must congratulate you. It's wonderful you're in the cast of *Darleen Come Home*. I know you'll do an excellent job."

"Thanks," I said, feeling a mite suspicious. Lonnie had a devious look about him.

"Pity Melodie's so upset, but she'll get over it."

"I hope so," I said. After a pause, I asked, "Is there something else?"

"Now you mention it, there is. You see, Pauline's got this ambition to be the most successful star wrangler in history. She wants to take Glowing Bodies to the top of the event coordinating universe."

"Good on her," I said. "Hope she makes it."

"That's where you come in."

I stared at him, astonished. "What?"

"No one's ever been able to wrangle Earl Garfield. He doesn't attend industry events, period. For event coordinators he's the holy grail, especially since he dates reclusive heiress Queenie Van Dorn. To deliver both of them to a major function would be an unbelievable coup."

I could see where this was going. "No way, Lonnie," I said firmly. "I'm not getting involved in the star wrangling business in any way, shape, or form."

Misery flooded Lonnie's face. "I've sort of promised Pauline you'd..."

"I'd what?"

"Please, Kylie, I'm pleading with you. Would you at least speak with Pauline. Please?"

"Lonnie—"

"I'll never ask another favor."

I looked at my watch. I'd be late if I didn't get going. "Tomorrow, let's—"

"Oh, thank you, Kylie!"

"Thank you? Hold on, Lonnie."

But he was already hurrying off. His last words, as he disappeared into the courtyard, were, "Pauline will be so pleased."

Strewth!

CHAPTER EIGHT

By the time I got back to the office, everyone was packing up to go home. "Any messages?" I said to Melodie. With icy disdain, she silently handed them to me. The first was from Ariana, saying she'd been delayed, but would definitely call in before she went home.

The second was a scrawled note from Brucie: *Hitting hot spots with Melodie tonight. Woo-hoo! Discuss Dingo sitch tomorrow.*

"Have a beaut time tonight," I said to her. Melodie gave a regal nod, her lips tightly compressed.

The third item was a hand-delivered letter addressed to both Ariana and me. There was no mystery about who it was from, as Norris Blainey's image, his smile close to a sneer, appeared under the return address. I reckoned this was the offer he'd mentioned. It didn't matter how large the sum, Kendall & Creeling would not be selling.

I had a fair idea I'd get hot under the collar if I read it, so I decided to wait and open the envelope with Ariana's cool presence to calm me.

Harriet paused on her way out. "What do you think of our new door chime?" she asked me.

"What new door chime?"

"Fran had it installed this afternoon. It plays a phrase from some Spanish song."

"Grenada," said Melodie to Harriet. "It's in keeping with the theme of the building."

Fran's Spanish mania was clearly out of control. As her humungous SUV hadn't been in the parking area when I'd arrived, I guessed she'd already left. I'd deal with her tomorrow.

Harriet said goodbye and maneuvered her hugely pregnant self out the front door. A second later she was back. "I forgot to ask, how did it go with Rosenblum?"

I didn't think it was fair to rub Melodie's nose in the fact I'd retained an entertainment lawyer, so I murmured, "Everything's jake, thanks."

This was to no avail. Melodie's eyes were mere slits. "Howie Rosenblum?" she inquired of Harriet in a tight tone. "The Howie Rosenblum?"

From Harriet's expression, she'd realized too late that this was a risky topic. "Gotta run," she said, moving out the front door as fast as her bulk allowed.

"I suppose I should be grateful you didn't try to take over Larry-my-agent," Melodie snarled.

This was progress. She was actually talking to me. "Fair dinkum," I said, "getting cast as Olive was because I just happened to be in the right place at the right time."

Melodie's eyes had gone from slits to wide-eyed outrage. "I've slaved at my craft for years. *Years*, Kylie. And yet you, with no training, no talent, and no burning drive to succeed in the biz…" She threw up her hands at the injustice of it all.

"I've got zero ambitions to be an actor."

"Oh, sure," said Melodie scathingly, "so that's why you went ahead with the audition." Using unnecessary force, she began to pack up her things, preparatory to leaving for the day. She paused to snap, "Just don't come crawling to me for help the first time you have to interpret the role and you fall flat on your face."

"I am a bit worried about that," I said.

She made a derisive sound. "What do you understand of the techniques for reaching deep within yourself to connect with your innermost primal store of fundamental emotions?" she inquired.

"Crikey, not much, so it's lucky I'm only in two episodes."

"Only two episodes, you say?" Melodie drew a shuddering breath. "Stellar careers have been launched on the strength of one episode in a series. And you have two. Two!"

Muttering to herself, she picked up her things and stomped towards the door. To placate her, I said, "No matter how many episodes Olive's in, there's not much risk of me launching a stellar career on *Darleen Come Home*, is there?"

"None," said Melodie. "Less than none. Less than less than none." She paused to consider, then added, "A two-headed Martian with no experience in the performing arts would have a better chance of a successful acting career than you."

* * *

When everyone had gone, I went in search of Julia Roberts. It was odd that she wasn't in evidence, as she had an impressively accurate internal clock that never failed to alert her to the fact that her dinner time was fast approaching.

I even checked Lonnie's room, just in case she had managed to sneak in and hide herself. "Jules? Are you lurking in here somewhere?"

I thought I heard a muffled but indignant yowl back in the direction of the kitchen. "Jules?"

Guided by increasingly irritated cries, I found myself in front of the disaster supplies storage room. When I opened the door, Julia Roberts shot out like a tawny rocket.

"How did you manage to get yourself shut in?" I asked. Jules didn't deign to answer, being busy soothing herself with a quick wash. "Fran is very thingie about the disaster supplies," I pointed out, "and she's likely to throw a wobbly if she finds out you've been in there."

Jules stopped washing and gave me a thoughtful look. "OK," I said, "it can be our little secret, but don't do it again."

My heart gave a happy leap as I heard the unmistakable sound of Ariana's footsteps in the hallway. I went to meet her, Jules following behind with her tail held confidently high.

Ariana looked absolutely drained. There were dark smudges under her blue eyes and lines of strain on her face. Without even considering she might reject the embrace, I walked up to her and put my arms around her. She leaned into me and I held her tight, my sharp delight tempered with concern.

"It's Natalie," she said against my shoulder. "Yesterday morning she collapsed. A stroke. I've been with her at the hospital ever since."

"Ariana, I'm so sorry."

This was a perilous subject. I didn't dare say more, although my head buzzed with questions. Was the stroke catastrophic or mild? Was Natalie conscious? What was the prognosis?

Alzheimer's had robbed Natalie of her memories and left Ariana in a limbo where the woman she loved was still physically present, but only faint flickers of her personality remained. If you gave me the choice, I'd die rather than exist in a life of gray confusion. Did Ariana think that too? Now that Natalie had suffered an additional assault upon the tissues of her brain, did Ariana wish the shell that remained of Natalie would give up and quietly slip away?

Inexplicably, a line of poetry I remembered from English class at Wollegudgerie High came to me: *I have been half in love with easeful Death.* It was Keats, I thought, and I hadn't really understood it then—I did now.

I dropped my arms as Ariana stepped back from me. She answered one of my questions by saying, "It was a moderately severe stroke that's affected her left side. I waited to speak with her doctor about results of the latest tests. Natalie's heart is strong. He expects her to survive."

I ventured to ask, "Does Natalie have any family?"

"No living relatives. Thank God that years ago we thought to get medical power of attorney for each other. If I didn't have that, I wouldn't be able to see her, or have any say in her treatment."

Feeling there was nothing else I could safely ask, I said, "Would you like something to drink? I haven't got any hard liquor, but I've got wine."

She didn't demur, as I expected, but simply said, "Thank you, yes."

Julia Roberts led the way to the kitchen, her ears at an impatient slant. I followed her with Ariana, thinking how bonzer it would be if I had a sitting area where the storage room now stood. If it existed, Ariana and I wouldn't have to perch on tall stools in the kitchen, but could luxuriate in comfortable lounge chairs. Blast Fran's obsession with Homeland Security's more alarmist recommendations. I approved of being prepared for unexpected crises, but not quite *that* prepared.

I must have muttered Fran's name, because Ariana said, "Fran? She's not still here, is she? When I was turning in through the gates, I thought I saw Quip sitting in a car on the other side of the road."

"She went home ages ago."

"Then I was mistaken. It wasn't Quip."

I'd left the letter from Norris Blainey on the kitchen counter, meaning to open it after dinner if Ariana hadn't come by. When I pointed the envelope out to her, she grimaced. "I'll fax the letter to Kenneth Smithson tomorrow. He'll be representing us in any communications with Blainey."

Julia Roberts had marched into the kitchen and made a beeline for her dish. Now she was directing an implacable stare in my direction. I hastened to provide liver and chicken, simmered, the label assured me, in its own delicious juices. "That smells good," said Ariana as I opened the can. "I must be hungry."

I knew she preferred red wine. "This is a tip-top Aussie Cabernet Sauvignon," I said, pouring two glasses.

Ariana rubbed her forehead and sighed. "This is going to knock me for a loop. I've had countless cups of hospital coffee, but I couldn't eat anything much."

"Steak and mashed potatoes? I can rustle that up in no time."

She gave me a tired smile. "That sounds wonderful."

While Ariana called her next-door neighbor to ask him to feed Gussie, Ariana's gorgeous German shepherd, I started dinner. I wasn't what you'd call a gourmet cook by any stretch, but I was OK with plain food.

I'd mastered the stove's griller, though oddly, the appliance booklet referred to it as a broiler. I had two filet steaks sitting in the refrigerator, as I'd bought them on the way home from meeting with Howie Rosenblum, thinking that I'd have to show Brucie some hospitality by cooking him at least one meal in the next few days. Brucie's loss would be Ariana's gain.

"I've only got frozen mashed potatoes to heat in the microwave," I said apologetically, "not the real thing made from scratch."

"Frozen is fine. I'm suddenly starving, so anything sounds appetizing to me."

Ariana wasn't joking. She devoured everything on her plate. "That was great. Thank you very much, Kylie."

For some reason my name seemed to hang in the air between us. Was it because her thanks had been expressed so formally? I didn't expect her to use an endearment—she never had, even in those few intensely exciting times when we'd been in bed together.

Perhaps she was distancing herself because all her love and attention was focused on Natalie. I wanted to say, "Please don't push me away," but instead I remarked casually, "A lot's happened while you've been out of the office. For instance, I've joined the cast of *Darleen Come Home.*"

A rare look of astonishment appeared on Ariana's face. "You're kidding me."

"I'm fair dinkum. It's been an eventful time, including a blue with Fran about the Spanish furniture. Do you want the short and sweet version, or all the gruesome details?"

"Pour me another glass of wine, then start at the beginning."

I began with Fran and the secret commission she'd scored for the furniture she was ordering off her own bat for the office. "I know I should have waited for you, Ariana, so we could talk to her together, but Fran really got my goat, telling me I had to have a new desk, when I didn't need or want one."

I told Ariana about Quip's novel, *I, Developer,* and the money problems Fran claimed had forced her to take desperate measures, and how even Quip didn't know about Fran's deal with Maximum Spanish.

Ariana's expression was severe. "Fran has no excuse for this. Her job's on the line. I hope you told her that."

Feeling embarrassed, I said, "Fact is, Fran played me for a mug. I found myself feeling sorry for her, instead of concentrating on what she'd done wrong."

"I'll deal with Fran tomorrow," said Ariana in a steely tone.

Not wanting her to dwell on my abject failure at managing the Fran situation, I skipped onto seeing Dingo O'Rourke at Bellina Studios that morning, and how on the way out I'd managed, quite by chance, to snag the part of Olive, Timmy's long-lost Aussie sister.

That got a soft laugh from Ariana. She shook her head. "It's extraordinary the things that happen to you." Her smile faded. "Correct me if I'm wrong, but wasn't Melodie auditioning for that very part?"

"Unfortunately, yes." I detailed how I'd prevaricated too long, so the receptionists' network had swung into action and given Melodie the bad news before I could. "She was furious, and I could cope with that, but when she started crying, I felt a bit grim." I described the deep freeze that followed, which was not helped by the fact that, thanks to Harriet, I now had an entertainment lawyer of some repute.

Ariana said with cool logic, "Melodie has no right to blame you. She missed out simply because she wasn't the best one for the role. The director made the judgment that you were. End of story."

"Melodie makes it clear she thinks I'm going to fizzle as Olive, and she could very well be right."

Ariana warmed me by saying, "I wouldn't be so sure."

"You think I'll ace it, and be discovered as the new great talent from Down Under. Not bloody likely!"

I went on to tell her how Cousin Brucie was in town, and dead set on helping me investigate what was going on with Dingo O'Rourke. That reminded me of the call from Phyllis Blake about the two odd blokes who'd been hanging around Dingo's apartment building. Ariana suggested one possibility was that Dingo was reneging on a gambling debt and these were enforcers, sent to persuade him to pay up. As she pointed out, fear of the consequences of non-payment would explain why Dingo was holed up in the safety of the studio lot.

I deliberately didn't mention my mum's latest crisis at the Wombat. Why tell Ariana how Mum had implored me for the zillionth time to come back home, and run the risk that Ariana would break my heart by saying that she now agreed I should return to Oz and leave the running Kendall & Creeling to her? As my mum would say, let sleeping dogs lie.

The final event of the day worth mentioning was how Lonnie had intercepted me in the car park and somehow managed to get the idea that I'd be willing to talk to Pauline Feeney about how she might achieve her ambition to be the star wrangler who wrangled the reclusive Earl Garfield.

"I wasn't being a pushover," I said hastily, in case she thought it was another example of me being a soft touch. "Lonnie just mistook what I said, and he left before I could set him straight."

With a sardonic smile, Ariana said, "I imagine Lonnie knew exactly what you said, and deliberately misunderstood you."

I drooped a bit at that. "I haven't got a rep for being a softy at home, but I seem to have become a gutless wonder since I came to Los Angeles."

Ariana started to say something, but a blast of *Grenada* startled us both.

"What's *that?*" she asked.

"It's our new door chime. Fran had it installed this afternoon while I was out."

Grenada sounded again. Ariana said something under her breath and strode towards the front door, with me hurrying to keep up with her. Whoever it was had given up on *Grenada* and was now loudly knocking.

"It's Norris Blainey," he bellowed through the door. "I know you're in there, and I'm not leaving until I speak with you both."

Because I'd been living here by myself, Lonnie had recently installed a security camera. Ariana checked the screen. "It is Blainey. He's alone."

A red rage swept through me. How dare this bloke come pounding on our door. I turned the lock and flung the door open. "Stop that!"

Norris Blainey had his fist raised, about to renew his knocking. For a weedy bloke, he made quite a racket. He was wearing a dark suit, white shirt, and red tie. An unpleasant grin spread over his face. "Good evening, ladies. Let's have a nice little chat about the offer for your property I arranged to be delivered this afternoon. As you can see, I've been generous—probably too generous, if truth be told—so I imagine it's an opportunity you'll be keen to take. I must warn you, my offer is time-sensitive, so you'll need to act decisively while it's on the table."

"Shove off." I was so furious, my voice was shaking.

In a tone as cool as her face, Ariana said, "Kenneth Smithson is our attorney. Any communications between you and Kendall & Creeling will go through his office. Now, Mr. Blainey, I must ask you to leave. You're trespassing on our property."

Blainey kept right on smiling. "Surely we can talk this over without involving lawyers. They cost an arm and a leg, and you'll get no better deal than you had at the beginning."

"Goodnight, Mr. Blainey," Ariana said, beginning to close the door in his face.

He moved quickly to shove it open again. "I haven't been successful in business by taking no for an answer," he said, stepping through the doorway.

I completely lost it. Blainey's grin disappeared as I grabbed him by his red silk tie, yanked him towards me, spun him around, and shoved his arm up his back until he squeaked. With a skill born of dealing with obstreperous drunks at The Wombat's Retreat—I only tried it with little blokes like Blainey—I marched him across the courtyard to his car, a big, showy Jaguar.

"You bitch," he said. "You'll pay for this."

I didn't say a word. Ariana joined me and we waited until he drove off.

We walked in silence back across the courtyard. Once inside, I said, "Sorry I did my nana...lost my temper. Do you think he'll have me for assault?"

Ariana gave me a small smile. "He refuses to leave when asked to, tries to force his way inside, and as a result is frog marched by a woman back to his car. I don't think Norris Blainey will be mentioning this to anyone, anytime soon."

CHAPTER NINE

Ariana was exhausted, and on top of that had had three glasses of wine. I didn't even try to persuade her to stay the night with me, but pointed out she was in no condition to get behind a wheel, so I would drive her home. After a token resistance she agreed to be chauffeured.

For security reasons the courtyard and parking area were brightly lit at night, so it would be impossible for Norris Blainey to lurk there undetected. Although I was sure he was long gone, he was a nasty piece of work, so I wouldn't put it past him to plot some form of revenge for his humiliation.

Ariana obviously had the same thought. As we walked to my car, I noticed her checking everything out, her hand in her pocket of her jacket.

"You carrying?" I said.

She grinned. "Great command of private-eye lingo. And yes, I am."

I knew that, having been a cop, Ariana hadn't found it too difficult to get a license to carry a concealed weapon. I had Buckley's chance, I reckoned, of being able to swing such a license, not that I was any good with handguns anyway. I'd grown up with rifles and shotguns and was a fair shot with both, but the law in Australia restricted the possession of handguns to law enforcement and a small number of private citizens with exceptional reasons to have such weapons.

Assured that no one was lurking and that nothing had been done to my car, we pulled out into Thursday night traffic. Sunset Boulevard was always busy, but starting from Thursday evening and going through to the early hours of Monday morning, the closer one got to the Sunset Strip nightlife, the more frantic it became.

We left the frenetic activity and drove up winding roads into the Hollywood Hills. Ariana sat silent beside me. I wanted to touch her, to comfort her, but of all people I was the one who couldn't. I would never say it aloud, but in a sense, Natalie was my rival, although she would never know I even existed. I'd compromise, gladly share Ariana with her, but that wasn't my decision to make.

I gave myself a sharp mental slap. While I was whinging to myself about the circumstances that made my relationship with Ariana problematic, she was grieving. In Ariana's memories Natalie lived, vibrant and alive, but in the reality of the here and now, she was a tragic figure, stricken in mind and body. How would I be coping if Ariana was the one lying in a hospital bed physically present, but with her intelligence and passion melted away, leaving only a husk behind?

Not recognizing the sound of my car, Ariana's German shepherd barked a warning when I pulled into the parking area behind Ariana's house. Poor Gussie had been left alone for one night already, and even though I knew a professional dog walker took her out every weekday, she must have been fretting for Ariana's presence.

Ariana called out Gussie's name, and the barking stopped immediately. We both got out of the car. Ariana looked at me. So there'd be no confusion between us, I said, "I'll see you inside, then I'll go. As your car's still at the office, what time do you want me to pick you up in the morning?"

"Eight? Would that be OK?"

"Right-oh. Eight it is."

She put a hand on my arm. "Kylie, thank you."

I felt awkward and a bit embarrassed. If Ariana could read my mind she'd know how much I wanted to come inside, to make love with her, to banish, if only for a few moments, every thought of grief and loss from her thoughts.

* * *

As instructed by Ariana, when I got back to Kendall & Creeling I double-checked the area before getting out of my car. No one was lying in wait for me. I expected, after everything that had happened, that I wouldn't sleep well, but as soon as my head touched the pillow I was unconscious, and didn't stir until the sound of the industrial-strength vacuum woke me up.

First impressions can be indelible, I'd found, particularly with our cleaner, Luis. He had never quite got over our initial meeting, when I'd appeared waving a golf club to defend myself against a supposed intruder, not knowing that he came very early several times a week to clean the offices.

For that reason I was always very circumspect with Luis. I tried to avoid walking up behind him and I kept a good bit of personal space between us when we spoke. Even with this care, he continued to treat me like an unpredictable and possibly deranged individual.

I showered and dressed, then headed for the kitchen to grab a quick breakfast before I picked up Ariana. Turning a corner, I almost ran into Luis, who started violently, then murmured something in Spanish, possibly an appeal to a saint for protection.

How ridiculous was this? A cleaner terrified of me, of all people? "G'day, Luis," I said in as friendly a tone as possible. "Nice weather we're having, don't you think?"

He nodded slowly, all the while looking at me warily.

"Look," I said, showing him my hands. "No golf club." He took a step back. I took a step forward. "Trust me," I said sincerely, "no weapons of any kind."

I'd been trying to pick up a little Spanish from a traveler's phrase book, since so many people spoke the language in LA. I gave Luis my version of: "Hello, my name is Kylie. How are you today?"

Perhaps my accent needed work, as Luis said, "I go," and rapidly went.

I was in the kitchen bolting down the last of my porridge when Lonnie appeared holding a McDonald's bag containing his customary fast-food breakfast. "Catch the news this morning?" he asked.

"Not yet. What's up?"

"The Collie Coalition has gone public. Threatened Darleen in particular and Bellina Studios in general, if their demands that Darleen be replaced with a pure-bred collie are not met."

He turned on the kitchen TV and flicked around stations until he found a local morning show. The story was top of the news.

"Beloved dingo Darleen of *Darleen Come Home* finds herself in peril this morning, Rod!" an anorexic, white-blond young woman exclaimed to a sleek bloke with blow-dried hair, a deep tan, and very white teeth.

His smile disappeared, replaced with a grave demeanor. "Peril indeed, Delia! A previously unknown group, calling themselves the Collie Coalition, using untraceable e-mails, have made grave but unspecified threats against Darleen and the studios where *Darleen Come Home* is produced. Their demands include the immediate replacement of Darleen with a collie dog."

"So sad!" exclaimed the blond. "Let's cross to Gloria on location."

The screen changed to show a rather windblown brunet clutching a microphone and looking intense. In the background I recognized the industrial street fronting the studios I'd visited the day before.

Gloria had the same breathless, hyper-enthusiastic delivery as the anchors at the station. "Delia, Rod, I'm at the fabled Bellina Studios, home of so many award-winning shows. Now a pall of fear and confusion lies over every soundstage. An atmosphere of pending peril is in the air. Earlier this morning, I spoke with renowned director Earl Garfield…"

The picture switched to a shot of a black limo drawing up to the entrance. As it slowed, Gloria galloped forward, microphone at the ready. She tapped on the window, calling out, "Mr. Garfield! Mr. Garfield! What are your feelings about these ominous threats to Darleen, the star of your show?"

The window slid partly down and Gloria shoved her microphone into the opening. Earl Garfield's face was barely discernible, and the two words he said were impossible to make out. Reading his lips, it appeared he had told her to get lost, using a more basic term.

Now Gloria was back on camera in the present. Shaking her head, she said, "Reclusive director Earl Garfield was far too upset to make a statement at this time, but it seems he has every confidence that the authorities will track and bring to justice the perpetrators. This is Gloria Soames, reporting from Bellina Studios. Back to you, Rod and Delia."

Rod and Delia had been joined at their elaborate desk by a solemn bloke with a crew cut and a badly fitting gray suit. Delia smiled at him with every evidence of deep delight. "And here with us this morning is our terrorism expert, Hadley Charles, author of the best-selling book on domestic terrorism, *Not If, But When*."

Rod chimed in with, "From your wide intelligence experience, Hadley, what can you tell viewers about the Collie Coalition?"

"They're an intensely secret organization, Rod, thought by some to have ties to terrorist groups outside the country. Al Qaeda has been mentioned."

Delia raised her eyebrows. "Really, Hadley? But there's been no statement this morning from the White House."

"My sources," snapped Hadley, obviously irritated to have his statement questioned, "tell me that the threat the Collie Coalition poses is, as we speak, being discussed at the highest levels of national security. The *highest* levels."

As the station went into one of its interminable commercial breaks, Lonnie said to me, "I told you, didn't I? Homeland Security are on the case, pity help us. Most of them wouldn't know if their pants were on fire."

* * *

I picked Ariana up at eight sharp. She was somber, but seemed rested. As I drove down from the Hills, she said, "I'll tell Bob about Natalie, and of course my sister will have told Fran this morning, but I'd rather no one else knows. Janette said she'd ask Fran not to discuss it in the office."

"Right-oh." I broke the silence that followed by saying, "*Darleen Come Home* was in the news this morning."

"I heard it on the radio."

"The intelligence expert I saw on television said there might be an Al Qaeda connection."

"It's highly unlikely. Here's a group whose stated aim is to have a collie replace a dingo on a TV show. It seems quite a stretch to paint them as linked to international terrorism."

"Lonnie says he's heard that Homeland Security is involved."

"That'll please Fran," said Ariana with an acerbic smile.

As I parked the car, I automatically checked the vehicles already there. I'd put Dad's Mustang away in the garage accessed by a lane at the back of the building, so it wasn't in view. Ariana's dark blue BMW was, of course, and Lonnie's nondescript Nissan was parked in his usual slapdash manner. Harriet's black VW Beetle was missing. Neither Fran's bulky SUV nor Melodie's red sports car had yet arrived, but Bob Verritt, who'd recently purchased a silver Lexus—his pride and joy—drove in behind us.

"Well, what do you think of our Kylie?" he said to Ariana as he got out of his car. "Trainee private eye, amateur architect, media star…the girl's got talent coming out her ears."

"Architect?" said Ariana, eyeing me. "You don't have some new plan, do you?"

"Nothing new," I said. "Just the sitting room I've mentioned before."

"Don't trust her," said Bob, grinning. "Turn your back for five minutes, and she'll have a wall down."

He walked with us into the building, still chuckling. Ariana said to me that we should speak to Fran about her underhanded deal with the furniture later today, after Ariana had caught up with the work that had piled up while she'd been absent.

She disappeared into her office and I went along to my room, deep in thought about Dingo O'Rourke. Now that the news was out about the Collie Coalition, maybe he could relax a bit, as surely all this publicity would make an attempted dingo-napping much more unlikely.

I opened my office door, and was astonished to see Quip lounging in a chair waiting for me. As usual, he was wearing a tight T-shirt to highlight the impressive physique he'd achieved with regular sessions at the gym.

"Quip? Is Fran here? I didn't see the SUV."

"I'm driving a rental. I left it on the street."

I remembered Ariana's remark that she thought she'd seen Quip sitting in a parked car near our gates. "You were there last night, weren't you?" I said.

His handsome face flushed with chagrin. "I didn't think anyone saw me."

"Ariana did. What were you doing?"

"Did Fran tell you I'm writing a novel?"

"Titled *I, Developer*, featuring Morris Rainey, a barely disguised portrait of Norris Blainey," I said.

"So you understand why I've been shadowing Blainey, hence the rental car. I'm gathering material for my book. I follow him everywhere he goes."

"Crikey, Quip, isn't that dangerous? He's got a rep as a mega-ruthless bloke."

Quip flexed a muscle or two. "You think he'd be any match for me?"

"I reckon he'd pay someone else to deal with you. He wouldn't get his hands dirty himself."

"I can handle it," said Quip, jutting his manly jaw. "Besides, I've got a contact in Blainey's office, so I'd get some warning if he was up to anything like that."

"The contact wouldn't be a receptionist, would it?"

I felt quite chuffed when Quip gazed at me with open admiration. "I can see you've got a handle on this detecting routine already," he said. Then his expression changed to one of concern. "Kylie, it's vital you don't mention my receptionist contact to Fran. Promise me you won't. She wouldn't understand."

I understood why he was worried. Fran was notably possessive. "Good-looking is she?" I asked. "And blond, I bet."

"Blond, yes. Good-looking, yes. But it isn't a she—it's a he."

I didn't comment. Fran and Quip's marriage was a mystery to me. Angels would possibly fear to tread in this area—I certainly did.

To fill the moment of awkward silence, I said, "Have you got any useful material, with all this lurking around?"

"Have I ever! Sensational stuff! Corruption, kickbacks, politicians in his pocket..." Quip gave me a brilliant smile. "Help me out here, Kylie. Give me word for word what Blainey said to you and Ariana last night. I heard him pounding on the door. I couldn't see clearly from behind the fence, but after a short time I did see you walk him to his car."

Obviously Quip hadn't realized I'd had Norris Blainey's arm up between his shoulder blades, and I wasn't going to admit to losing my temper, so I said vaguely, "He didn't say much. He mentioned how generous the offer he was proposing was, we basically said we weren't interested and asked him to leave."

Disappointed, Quip asked, "No swearing? No threats? I need the raw immediacy of the real-life interactions to make my protagonist, Morris Rainey, live and breathe."

"Can't say there were, not really." As I said this I remembered the venom in Blainey's voice when he'd choked out the words, *You bitch. You'll pay for this.*

* * *

After Quip left, clearly dissatisfied with the quality of information on Blainey I could supply, I spent an hour answering e-mails and getting my files up to date. Then I decided a cup of tea would hit the spot, so I headed for the kitchen. I came through the door to find Fran, Harriet, and Lonnie already there.

"Someone shut Julia Roberts in the storage room holding the disaster supplies," Fran was saying in a militant tone. "Melodie says it wasn't her, so which one of you was it?"

"Not me," said Lonnie far too quickly. We all looked at him.

Fran fixed Lonnie with a basilisk stare. "Why did you do that, Lonnie?"

"What makes you think it was me? You know I'm allergic. I do everything I can to keep away from that cat."

Harriet said helpfully, "Earlier, I saw Julia Roberts pawing at the door. Perhaps she managed to open it herself."

Fran didn't shift her gaze from Lonnie. "You let that cat into the storage area, didn't you?"

Lonnie shot out a mutinous lower lip. "So what if I did? What was the harm? I figured if Julia Roberts was in the disaster supplies, that meant she wasn't trying to get into my room."

"The harm," snapped Fran, "was that she managed to open a container and make herself a nest in what were previously sterile field dressings. Dressings, I might remind you, that are essential in the treatment of the seriously wounded."

"Cats love boxes," I said. "It's natural she'd want to get in one. And Jules wouldn't have known they were sterile field dressings."

"Fran! Fran! Come quick!" Breathless, Melodie ricocheted into the kitchen.

Fran scowled. "What the hell is the matter with you?"

"It's not me," Melodie gasped. "It's Quip. He's hurt. There's blood everywhere!"

CHAPTER TEN

"It was nothing," said Brucie modestly, leaning with a nonchalant air against Melodie's fake-Spanish desk. "I came upon two yobbos beating the living daylights out of a bloke, so of course I waded in."

Melodie gazed at him with something approaching adoration. "Oh, Bruce, that was so brave of you."

He gave her an unassuming smile. "Thanks, but anyone would have done the same."

I recalled that Brucie had played on the Wollegudgerie footie team and had never been afraid of a bit of biffo. This was fortunate for Quip, who'd been ambushed in our parking area. But for Brucie's intervention, he would have sustained even more damage than he had.

The ambulance had left with Fran accompanying a semi-conscious Quip. He had a broken nose, eyes swollen almost shut, and a split lip, and possibly a couple of cracked ribs. The hospital ER would ascertain if he had any more serious injuries.

The cops had been called, of course, and Ariana had dealt with them. They'd interviewed Brucie, who hadn't been able to give much more than a vague description of the two thugs because they'd bolted the moment it was clear Brucie was more than they could handle.

The phone rang and Melodie picked up. "Lexus, hi! Can't talk. Call you back, OK?"

"That Lexus," Brucie said with a reminiscent grin, "she sure knows how to party."

Lexus—actually Cathy, but she'd changed her name to something she considered more upmarket—shared an apartment with Melodie.

"So Lexus joined you and Melodie painting the town red last night, did she?"

"Bright red! Lexus is a bit of all right, I can tell you."

Melodie frowned, obviously not too happy to hear this glowing description of her flatmate. She opened her mouth to say something, but the phone rang again. "Taylor? Hi! Yes, *awesome*. And the blood!" She looked at Brucie. "He's right here. An Aussie. Can't talk now. Call you back. Bye."

Another call came through. "Mandy, hi! Like, just outside the door. His face? Mask of blood. But can't talk now. Call you back."

It was clear that the news of Quip's bashing and Brucie's intervention was already burning the lines of the receptionists' network.

Almost immediately, the phone rang again. "Yancy, hi! Yes, you heard right. Ambulance just left. No, I can't talk now"—she looked meaningfully at me and Brucie—"because I'm not alone…"

"Come on," I said, taking Brucie's arm, "Melodie has some serious networking to do." I'd only taken a few steps down the hall before it struck me. "Hang on for a mo, Brucie."

"Bruce!"

"Sorry. *Bruce*. I have to ask Melodie something…"

I went back to the reception desk. "Melodie?"

"Hold for a sec, Yancy." She looked at me impatiently. "Yes?"

"Yancy's a man's name."

"So? Yancy's a man."

"And Yancy's a receptionist?"

She gave an irritated sigh. "There's a sprinkling of male receptionists around town. A couple are quite good."

"Yancy wouldn't work for Norris Blainey's company, would he?"

Now Melodie was seriously peeved with me. "Receptionists shouldn't be judged by the companies they work for," she said sharply.

"I wasn't judging Yancy. I want to talk to him. Will you put him through to my office, please?"

The question of why I wanted to talk to Yancy trembled on Melodie's lips, but wisely she didn't put it into words.

"I have to take a call," I said to Brucie. "Why don't you check on Lonnie?"

When Melodie had appeared with the news that Quip had been hurt, Lonnie had hurried up to reception with everyone else. Big mistake. He'd taken one look at Quip slumped in a chair, his face covered with blood, had gone weak-kneed and had to be helped to a chair himself.

When Lonnie had recovered enough to wobble his way to his office, Bob had kindly escorted him to his door and seen him safely settled at his computer. Since then, there'd been no sign of Lonnie at all.

I expected Brucie to say something disparaging about Lonnie, along the lines that he was a sook for nearly fainting at the sight of blood, but Brucie was surprisingly sympathetic. "One look at a hypodermic and everything goes gray and I fall over. Just have to see a doc's white coat, and I feel woozy. It's embarrassing, but I can't help it. So I get what the bloke's been through."

With Brucie safely dispatched in Lonnie's direction, I zipped into my office to take the call. Julia Roberts, who'd obviously been seriously inconvenienced by all the activity this morning, was curled up in my chair. She was quite put out when I gently tipped her onto the floor.

"Yancy? This is Kylie Kendall."

"Hi, Kylie. Quip's spoken about you," he said with professional receptionist enthusiasm. With a note of real concern, he added, "Melodie says he's been badly hurt."

I visualized Yancy as Quip had described him—blond and good-looking. His voice didn't match my mental picture, though, as I always associated deep bass tones like his with dark hair.

I described Quip's injuries. "Fran's with him. We'll know more later, when she calls from the hospital."

"I warned him, you know. I said Blainey could be ruthless."

"Can you be overheard?" I asked, thinking it wouldn't help Yancy's job security to be badmouthing his boss.

"It's OK. I'm on my cell and I've ducked out of the building."

"So you're sure Norris Blainey is behind this?" I asked.

"Of course. Aren't you?"

"I can't think of anyone else who would harm Quip."

"Quip's such a rank amateur, as far as surveillance is concerned," Yancy said. "It was only a matter of time before something like this happened. Of course, it could've been worse. He could be dead. That would shut him up for good."

Bashing was one thing, murder quite another. "Are you fair dinkum? Norris Blainey would actually be involved in killing Quip just because Quip's writing a novel about him?"

"Blainey's been involved in mysterious deaths before. Why not again?"

Crikey, this was getting really hairy. "Yancy, you need to speak to the cops investigating Quip's bashing."

"No way! No cops. And I'll deny I said anything to you at all, if you give my name to them."

"But why?" Then I realised I was talking to myself. Yancy had hung up.

Brucie, hands in pockets, strolled into my room. "Hey, Lonnie has some seriously cool stuff," he said. "He could set himself up as a spy, no worries."

My phone rang. Maybe it was Yancy, calling back to say he'd had second thoughts about the cops.

"Oh, hello, Aunt Millie."

Brucie took his hands out of his pockets quick smart, and made frantic gestures to catch my attention. "Don't tell Mum I'm here," he mouthed.

"Brucie?" I said. "Yes, I've seen him. He's looking good. Actually, Aunt Millie, you'll be pleased to hear your son's a hero. Saved someone being viciously attacked."

Being a proud mother, albeit a pessimistic one—"Brucie could have been killed, maimed!"—my aunt demanded every last detail. I was well into a vivid depiction of Quip's beating and Brucie's bravery when I realized with dismay that Aunt Millie would rush to tell my mum about it, and in the process probably blow up the story into a full-scale battle. Major bummer! This was going to give Mum even more ammunition for her campaign to snatch me from the appalling dangers of Los Angeles and return me to the safety of outback Wollegudgerie.

I remembered to ask about Mum's crisis in the Wombat's kitchen. This started my aunt on a tirade.

"Jack O'Connell's a complete boofhead," she declared. "He lords it over the staff telling them how to do their jobs, when he's got no idea what he's talking about. Then he wonders why they get upset. I've told your mother, get rid of him. Jack's not worth the trouble. But will she?" Aunt Millie snorted. "Says she likes a man around the house. Jack's a poor excuse for a man, I told her. You can do better."

When I finally got Aunt Millie off the phone, I became aware that Brucie was scowling at me. "I had to tell your mum how you saved Quip," I said. "She would have heard anyway. And besides, you really were terrific, coming to his rescue like you did."

"It's not that," he snapped. "It's that I've had it with Brucie. The name's Bruce. Got it?"

"Got it. Sorry, but you've been Brucie all my life." To lighten the mood, I added brightly, "Did you know before he changed it, Quip's name was Bruce?"

"He went from Bruce to *Quip?*"

"He's a writer. It was a marketing decision."

"If I'd known," said my cousin, "I never would have saved him."

* * *

"How are you going?"

Lonnie looked up from his computer screen. "Your cousin Bruce is a great guy," he said. "Told me how he himself faints at the sight of a needle. Didn't feel quite such a fool, then."

Hell's bells! Brucie—Bruce—was making favorable impressions left, right, and center. I couldn't possibly have been wrong about him all these years. Maybe he'd had a personality transplant.

"What's the latest on Quip?" Lonnie asked.

"Fran's going to call as soon as she knows."

Lonnie shook his head. "I can't help thinking he set himself up for this. Quip's idea of how to conduct surveillance is laughable." Lonnie's expression became indignant. "And he wouldn't take my advice, and I *am* an expert in the field."

"Did he tell you why he was following Norris Blainey?"

"Some cockamamie idea about writing a novel. A novel! You're a screenwriter, I said, but Quip insisted he wanted total creative control and only a novel would give him that." Lonnie snorted. "Half the screenwriters in town want to write a novel, and half the novelists want to write a screenplay. Stick to what you know, I say!"

For some reason, Lonnie was getting quite het up over the whole thing. To calm him down, I said, "What advice about surveillance did you give Quip?"

"I said to him he didn't have to put himself in harm's way by getting so close to the subject. I even offered to set him up with a few basic things—a directional microphone to begin with, so he could pick up conversations at a distance. But would he? No. Quip had some idea he was like one of those old-time private eyes in a Raymond Chandler detective story."

"A white knight walking the mean streets, fighting evil?"

"Something like that," Lonnie said derisively.

"I've been talking to someone who works for Norris Blainey," I said. "The word is that in the past, Blainey has somehow been involved in mysterious deaths. Could you check it out?"

Lonnie frowned. "I seem to remember something…I'll get back to you."

The phone burped. Being Lonnie, an ordinary ring was too boring, so he'd set his up to sound as if the handset had a serious digestive problem.

"This will be Pauline," he said. "I told her to call before she saw you, so Julia Roberts could be safely locked away to protect Upton and Unity."

The phone burped again. "Before you answer that," I said, "I didn't agree to see her today. You just wanted to believe I had."

Lonnie's face went an unbecoming shade of puce. "Forgive me, Kylie. But you're not going to cancel, are you? Please, it means so much to me."

"Right-oh, I'll see her, but I'm not locking Julia Roberts away. It's her home, not the poodles'. Tell Pauline to walk around the building and meet me in the back garden." I added wickedly, "You can provide refreshments for us, Lonnie. And no flavored tea!"

On my way to the back door, I looked into Ariana's room. "Any word from Fran yet?"

Ariana glanced up from the folder she was reading. The blue of her eyes gave me a pleasant, familiar jolt. "Nothing yet."

"Pauline Feeney's in the backyard with Unity and Upton."

Ariana raised an eyebrow.

"Her standard poodles. She claims Jules terrorized them on Tuesday, which is hardly fair. It is Jules's home, after all. If Pauline wants to see me, it's the backyard or nothing."

Amused, Ariana said, "I see you're toughening up."

"I'm following your example," I said. "You're sort of a role model in toughness for me."

I was inordinately pleased when that made her laugh.

* * *

"G'day," I said to Pauline Feeney. She inclined her head in acknowledgement. "G'day Unity," I said to the black poodle. "And g'day Upton," I said to the white. He had shaved patches on his neck and back, no doubt from his run-in with Jules.

Pauline Feeney had seated herself at the redwood table I'd bought for the backyard. I'd referred to it as the back garden to Lonnie, but that was too grand a name for the area, which now, because of Fran's blasted disaster fixation, had a green shed housing all the office supplies displaced from the storage room.

Today Pauline's black hair had a blond streak. Her face, as before, was dead white, and her lips hectic red, her long fingernails the same shade. She wore a tight black jumpsuit with very high heels. Both she and Unity had matching jeweled collars, but because of Upton's injuries, his neck was bare.

"I've heard Quip Trent was in some sort of altercation," she said in her high, soft voice.

"From your receptionist at Glowing Bodies?" I asked, sure of the answer.

"Perhaps. Was he badly hurt?"

"We're waiting to hear."

She tilted her head reflectively. "His wife's an odd woman."

"Fran?"

"She came to me saying she was acting as an agent for her husband. Offered his services to Glowing Bodies. Said he had contacts we could use."

From her expression I gathered the offer had been unacceptable. "You turned her down?"

Pauline shrugged. "He knew lower-level celebrities only. No one we could use."

The source of Fran's sudden animosity towards Pauline Feeney was now obvious.

Lonnie came out the back door. He beamed at Pauline, and leaned over to kiss her cheek. "Coffee? Something to drink?"

She indicated Upton, who was peering nervously through the open door. "Nothing for me, but iced water for Upton, please. His nerves are shot to pieces."

"Be right back."

"Upton has required psychological counseling," Pauline said to me. "Like most pure-bred poodles, he is exceptionally sensitive. The last thing he expected was an ambush by that cat of yours."

"I've agreed to pay all Upton's vet bills," I said.

"Intensive therapy is very expensive. And he's going to need it for some time."

Stone the crows! How much was this going to cost?

"But," said Pauline, "you don't have to pay a cent, if you do one small favor for me."

"And that would be?"

"*Darleen Come Home* is a closed set. All I'm asking is you find some way to get me in. I'll do the rest."

* * *

When I came back inside after seeing Pauline Feeney off in her Cadillac Escalade, Melodie said, each word an ice cube, "It's your entertainment lawyer calling."

Yesterday, when I'd gone to his office in Century City, Howie had turned out to be super-friendly, in a snappy, let's-get-on-with-it sort of way. "Call me Howie," he'd said as he bounced over, smiling, and pumped my hand. "Love you

Aussies! Had some great times fishing for marlin off the coast of Queensland."

When he came on the line, Howie was just as briskly cheerful as the day before. He assured me how hard he'd fought on my behalf for a reasonable contract. The terms were now satisfactory, so he was having it delivered to Kendall & Creeling by courier this afternoon for my signature.

I'd pretty much thrown myself on Howie's mercy yesterday, so he'd given me a rapid-fire description of series television, including who was who on a soundstage and what I was to expect as a member of the cast. It'd soon become obvious that I was totally out of my depth, so Howie arranged for one of his junior staff members to liaise with the studios on my behalf. Now he had my schedule, plus various must-know and must-do items, which he'd courier to me with the contract.

"First up," Howie said, "you report Monday morning for a session with a dialogue coach to get your accent right."

"But I've got a dinky-di Aussie accent already!"

Howie laughed. "Roll with it, honey. Do whatever you're told. Don't argue."

After he'd rung off, I sat with my head spinning with all the information I needed to get straight. A dizzying number of people seemed involved in getting a TV show made. Howie had advised me to concentrate on those people I'd deal with directly, and stay out of the way of everyone else. "And don't get on the wrong side of the crew," he'd said. "Things can get very nasty if you do."

Maybe there was a TV industry equivalent to my PI bible, *Private Investigation: The Complete Handbook*. Because LA was the self-styled entertainment capital of the world, it stood to reason any big bookshop would have a section devoted to movies and TV. I was checking my watch, wondering whether I should nip out right now, when Ariana knocked.

"I've heard from Fran," she said. "The news is good. Nothing life-threatening. Quip's concussed, but no broken ribs, just bad bruising, and no internal injuries. The hospital's keeping him overnight for observation, but only as a precaution."

"I reckon we won't be hauling Fran over the coals today," I observed. Remembering how the normally unflappable Fran had been close to hysterical when she saw her wounded husband, I added, "Probably not for a good while, since she's so upset."

"Her day of reckoning is briefly postponed, not cancelled," said Ariana emphatically.

"I'm not being soft again," I protested.

"You are," she said, but it was with a smile.

Encouraged by her smile, I said, "About this weekend..."

"I'll be seeing Natalie." Ariana's voice was cool.

"I know you will be, but not twenty-four hours a day."

My heart swelled with pity and with fear. Something must have showed on my face, because Ariana's expression changed.

I thought, inconsequentially, *I could drown in the blue of your eyes.*

I said, my voice hardly above a whisper, "Let me comfort you."

"Kylie..."

"Ariana."

We stood looking at each other.

"Thank you," Ariana said.

CHAPTER ELEVEN

Much to my surprise Mum didn't call on Friday, although I knew Aunt Millie wouldn't have been able to resist boasting about Brucie's heroism. I could only hope that my mother had become so desensitized by the apparently endless procession of violent events in Los Angeles featured in Aussie newscasts that Quip's bashing didn't particularly register.

Melodie and Lexus were spending the weekend showing Brucie the LA sights, so I didn't have to worry about entertaining him.

I spent a leisurely breakfast reading the fat Saturday morning edition of the *Los Angeles Times*. Darleen the dingo's perilous situation had made the front page, and the entertainment section covered the story from the point of view of industry insiders. In one interview, Dustin Jaeger, who starred as Timmy in *Darleen Come Home*, stated that he was "devastated and shocked" that anyone could even think of harming Darleen, who was a sweet, affectionate dingo he was honored to count among his closest friends.

After breakfast I returned to the big chain bookstore where I'd purchased my invaluable handbook on private eyeing, and discovered they had a comprehensive section on television and movies. I spent ages going through the shelves, finding information and guidance covering every possible facet of the entertainment industry. The brightly colored covers fervently assured me that future success was certain, if I was to purchase the book. I could become a sought-after actor, or the writer of an award-winning screenplay, or the producer/director of a successful independent movie, no sweat.

I finally settled on one of the less flashy offerings, titled *A Beginner's Guide to Making TV Shows*. I didn't want to make a total galah of myself on the *Darleen* set, so by Monday I intended to have at least a rough idea of who did what in the making of a TV series.

When I got home I made myself a cup of tea and sat down with Julia Roberts to study the material Howie had sent me and the book I'd just purchased. TV production seemed to involve an awful lot of people. Soon I was deep into the roles and responsibilities of the executive producer, show runner, head writer, director, unit production manager, story editor, director of photography, script supervisor…And many had designated assistants—the director had two who alternated. Then there was the crew—gaffers, best boys, boom operators, sound mixers, camera operators…

"I'll never get all this stuff straight," I commented to Julia Roberts. She blinked, then yawned, the feline equivalent of a shrug. "You're so right, Jules," I said, "I will take Howie's advice, and roll with it."

Ariana had said she would be spending most of the day at the hospital with Natalie, but that she'd be home in the late afternoon. Would I be happy watching a movie on DVD and eating pizza?

Didn't she realize I'd be happy with anything, as long as I had her company?

I accepted as casually as she had offered the invitation. "I'll be there."

Ariana had said she'd be home by five at the latest. When I pulled into the parking area by her house at five-fifteen, I saw her sister Janette's white Volvo SUV. I heard a warning bark from Gussie as I got out of my car, then Janette opened the front door. Beside her Gussie grinned a welcome.

"Kylie, come in. Ariana called, she's been delayed." She stepped aside to let me past. "I've just delivered Gussie home. I've had her with me all day running the legs off my dachshund, Dutch."

It would be obvious to anyone that Janette and Ariana were sisters. Janette had the same pale hair as Ariana, although her blue eyes were not as vivid and she was carrying more weight. They differed most in personality. Where Ariana was detached, Janette was warm and friendly.

Janette was an artist of some note, specializing in disturbing, disconcerting images. At first glance, the scenes she depicted in almost photographic detail in her paintings seemed unexceptional. A closer look always showed something was very wrong—perhaps a human head was stacked neatly with logs in a fireplace, or a human finger, complete with blood-red nail polish, was being used as a bookmark.

Janette led the way into Ariana's beautiful living room, where a wall of glass provided a panoramic view of Los Angeles.

"Can I get you something to drink? Coffee? A soda?"

I didn't feel like anything, but I felt awkward, so to give me something to do with my hands, I said, "A Coke?"

"Coming right up."

When we were seated, each with tall glass of Coca-Cola, we silently regarded the stunning view. From this height, the sheer size of Los Angeles was evident. I tried to imagine what this huge basin, bounded by mountains and edged by the sea, would have looked like thousands of years ago.

Pulling my attention back to Janette, I said, "How is Quip?"

"He's stiff and sore, but safely home with Fran looking after him." She laughed. "Spare a thought for the poor boy. My daughter's no Florence Nightingale. She has the bedside manner of a pit bull."

I hesitated, then said, "And Natalie?"

Janette's grin faded. "No change. I don't know if Ariana told you, but Natalie's stroke was the less common one. It wasn't a clot, but a blood vessel breaking. There are aggressive treatments now for strokes caused by blood clots, but there's not as much that can be done for bleeding into the brain."

I decided to be direct. "I'm not sure what to say to Ariana. She's so cool, so contained."

Janette gave me an understanding smile. "My sister's always been rather reticent and the events in the past have accentuated her reserve. It might help you understand if you realize how Natalie's illness isolated Ariana. Natalie was much older than Ariana, and a professor at UCLA, so from the beginning the majority of their friends came from academia. Ariana was in the closet at the LAPD, which at that time was a hostile workplace for gays, so she formed very few close relationships there."

"My father was one."

Affection flooded Janette's face. "Colin was a wonderful man. I still can't believe he's gone. I'll always miss him."

I blinked hard, hoping Janette didn't see the sudden tears in my eyes. I missed him, too. He'd died before I'd really got to know him.

Janette went on, "When the unmistakable signs of Alzheimer's appeared, Natalie took early retirement. She had always been rightly proud of her intellect, so she was embarrassed and confused when it began to increasingly fail her. She became a recluse, withdrawing from almost everyone in their social network. I know Ariana tried to maintain friendships of her own, but she had so little time. Her life became filled with the demands of her career as a cop and her caretaker role with Natalie

I said, "Ariana's told me how she stayed close to my dad and how he offered her a partnership in his business."

"Colin admired Ariana for the way she managed her commitment to Kendall & Creeling while coping with Natalie's worsening mental state. And he was there for her when it became obvious that Natalie had deteriorated to the point where she needed to be in an intensive-care home."

"Making that decision must have been hard," I said inadequately.

"Devastating. It broke Ariana's heart, but at least she had me and Colin to support her. When Colin died, that left only me to confide in. Then you came along."

"I don't think I could say Ariana confides in me."

Janette leaned forward and put a hand on mine. "I'm so pleased you're in her life, Kylie. You make her laugh, and that's more of an achievement than you can imagine."

I said ruefully, "It's more laughing at me than with me."

"Don't sell yourself short. You're the only one, besides me, who can get close to her."

"Crikey, Janette, I don't know if I can claim that degree of intimacy."

Janette sat back with a knowing smile. "Really? That's not how I heard it from Ariana."

I felt myself blushing. "What did she say?"

"She said you were like no one she had ever met before. That you went to bed together. That she was astonished and disconcerted." Janette chuckled. "And that it was pretty damn good."

Flustered and delighted and confused, all at once, I blurted out, "I'm in love with her."

Janette's face softened. "Kylie, that may not be such a good idea."

"Why? Because Natalie will always be between us?"

"Ariana is fiercely loyal."

"I can't help how I feel. I don't want to help it." For the second time in a few minutes I felt tears sting my eyes. I was becoming such a sook. "You're saying I've got Buckley's, are you?" I asked.

She frowned. "Buckley's?"

"Meaning I've no chance." I added for clarification, "It's hopeless."

Her expression concerned, she said, "Ariana didn't mention any of this to me. Does she know how you feel?"

"Yes."

Gussie, who'd settled down near us, suddenly leapt joyfully to her feet, her plumed tail wagging.

"Ariana's home," said Janette.

We heard the key in the door and then the sounds of Gussie's enthusiastic greeting. Janette said to me in a soft voice, "Be careful with her, Kylie. When she called to say she was running late, it was because she couldn't drive. She was too upset. She didn't say why, but of course it's to do with Natalie."

Ariana and Gussie came into the room. Janette went to her and gave her a hug. "How's it going, sis?"

"OK." Ariana looked over Janette's shoulder at me. "Hi."

"Hello." I felt a fool, not sure of what to say or how to act. Janette took the pressure off by bustling around looking for her car keys.

Keys located, she gave Ariana another quick hug. "I'll speak with you tomorrow. If you want me to take Gussie again, just give the word." She flashed a smile at me. "See you, Kylie."

Ariana and Gussie went outside to see Janette off, leaving me in unexpected turmoil, uncertain of whether to ask Ariana about Natalie, or avoid the subject. Would it hurt her or help her to talk about it? Was I presuming too much? Why would she want to share her grief with me?

Let me comfort you, I'd said yesterday, confident that I could. Today I wasn't sure of anything.

* * *

In the end, we didn't watch a movie, but had pizza delivered and chatted about different things, none of which was remotely connected to Natalie. I did most of the talking. I amused her with my description of Pauline Feeney's ire when I'd told her there was no way I could get her onto the *Darleen* set. I told her about my conversation with Yancy and how he'd claimed his boss, Norris Blainey, some time in the past had been associated with mysterious deaths. I described my trepidation about embarking on an acting career, even though it was only for a short time and in a good cause, and how I expected Harry and Gert O'Rourke to call any minute, demanding to know what I'd found out about their son, Dingo, which so far would be nothing.

After we'd cleared away the remains of the pizza, we sat on either end of the couch with tea (me) and coffee (Ariana) looking out at the lights of the city.

Ariana broke the silence. "Sorry. I'm not very good company tonight."

I took a deep breath. "Do you want to talk about Natalie?"

"What is there to say?" I didn't speak. Ariana looked over at me. After a moment, she said, "Natalie doesn't know who I am."

How could anyone forget those laser blue eyes?

Ariana's lips trembled. "She's in restraints. She doesn't understand what's happened to her, and she keeps trying to get up, saying she wants to go home. Natalie means our house, where we lived in Santa Monica."

Ariana put her face in her hands. "When I was leaving, she pleaded with me, begged me to take her there. She said someone was waiting for her. Someone who loved her."

I put my tea down carefully, and moved to take her in my arms. I could cry for the pity of it, but that would be no comfort for Ariana. "What else?" I said.

"That was the worst. That and her bewilderment at not being able to get up and walk. She treated me like a friendly stranger. "Something's the matter," she said. "Will you get someone to help me, please?"

We sat in silence, Ariana in my arms, for a long time. Then she stirred. "I'm exhausted."

I kissed her, gently. She didn't push me away, nor did she respond. I said, "Come to bed."

"Kylie, sex is the last thing on my mind."

"I had more in mind a comfortable cuddle."

She gave me a small, tired smile. "Why do I not believe you?"

"Fair dinkum, Ariana. I won't start anything. Promise. It's just that I don't think you should be alone tonight."

She nodded slowly. "Just for tonight, I'd…"

"Appreciate my company?"

"Something like that."

"Can you give me an old T-shirt to wear? I hadn't planned ahead."

"Sure."

She moved without her usual taut energy. I took Gussie outside for a quick run, then came in, cleaned my teeth in the guest bathroom and changed into the old, soft T-shirt Ariana had left out for me. I padded into her bedroom. I could hear her shower still running, so I sat on the bed and waited.

She came out wearing green silk pajamas. I looked at her without passion, but with a love so overwhelming it frightened me. I clenched my teeth to avoid saying, "I absolutely adore you."

She turned back the bedspread, and without a word, we slid between the sheets. She reached up, snapped off the lamp beside the bed and turned her back to me. I put my arm around her and snuggled up close. Her breathing slowed almost immediately, and I realized she had fallen into an exhausted sleep.

I was sure I'd lie awake all night, joyful that Ariana lay within the circle of my arm. That was my last waking thought.

Sometime during the night I awoke. From her ragged breathing, I knew Ariana was weeping. I touched her wet face, then gently took her in my arms. Eventually I felt her relax as sleep overtook her again. This time I did lie awake for a long time.

* * *

"Night on the town, eh?" Lonnie said, beaming as he joined me at Kendall & Creeling's front door at eight-thirty the next morning. I gave him the hairy eyeball, and he said, "Sorry, Kylie. None of my business."

As I unlocked the door I thought how astonished Lonnie would be if he knew I'd spent the night in Ariana's bed. Or perhaps he wouldn't be at all surprised. His little-boy manner made it easy to underestimate how sharp he was.

Ariana had been sound asleep when I'd woken up. I'd shushed Gussie, let her outside for a bathroom break while I dressed, checked that Ariana was still sleeping, then put Gussie back inside with whispered instructions not to wake her mistress.

Lonnie was clutching his McDonald's breakfast, and was in an excellent mood, even side-stepping Julia Roberts without his usual complaints, when she darted out from behind Melodie's desk and tried to brush against his legs. Whistling, he made his way to the kitchen, where he busied himself making coffee, while I put the electric kettle on for tea.

It wasn't unusual for Lonnie to come in to work during the weekend, as up to now he hadn't had much of a personal life to take up his time. Come to think, he did look rather tattered around the edges, so I said, "I reckon you're the one who's had a night on the town."

"I did tie one on," he said, clearly pleased with himself. "In fact, I've hardly had any sleep at all. Out on Friday until the wee small hours, and last night Pauline took me to an event to launch a new perfume—Moonlight Reconnaissance. Everyone who's anyone was there."

He started to reel off names. I interrupted with, "Moonlight Reconnaissance is the name of a perfume?"

"Not exactly a perfume—a male fragrance. 'Moonlight' has connotations of romance and 'Reconnaissance' conjures up the raw, masculine element."

He shoved his face near mine. "Take a sniff. I'm wearing the Moonlight Reconnaissance aftershave splash and skin invigorator. What do you think?"

I sniffed. "Crikey," I said, "you're telling me a true blue bloke would wear *that?*"

He grinned at me. "It is a bit on the strong side, isn't it? But Pauline likes it." A calculating look crossed his face. "About Pauline—now that there's so much publicity about the Collie Coalition and the threat to harm Darleen, it's even more important that Pauline—"

"Don't ask, Lonnie. I've already told her there is no way, even without her poodles, I could get her onto the *Darleen Come Home* soundstage. She even suggested hiding in the boot of my car, but I pointed out security was checking every vehicle and she'd be sprung before she got through the gates."

"Pauline will find a way," Lonnie said, his admiration obvious. "She's implacable, relentless."

"Ruthless, even?"

"That too, but in a nice sense," Lonnie assured me. "And speaking of ruthless, what I've discovered so far about Norris Blainey is *very* interesting."

Dramatic pause. He waggled his eyebrows at me. Obediently I asked, "What was very interesting?"

"What happened to Louie and Louise Thorburn."

"They came to no good?"

"You could say that. They're both dead."

My skin prickled. "Murdered?"

"Hit and run. The vehicle was never found and no one was ever charged." Lonnie unwrapped his first Egg McMuffin and took a healthy bite. He chewed, swallowed, then sighed with satisfaction. "This is such good stuff. You should try it."

"I have. I prefer porridge. Now tell me about Norris Blainey."

Lonnie demolished the rest of the McMuffin, then said, "Blainey's always had a keen interest in show business, which isn't unusual. You'll find many entrepreneurs are lured by the glamour of Tinseltown, and this guy was no exception. He put money into a few projects, and finally linked up with a husband-and-wife team, Louie and Louise Thorburn, who'd previously produced TV programs. As three equal partners, they formed a production company called Zurial Entertainment. Blainey provided the funding, the Thorburns the expertise."

While Lonnie attacked his second McMuffin, I poured my tea. Fortified, he continued, "Initially Zurial Entertainment had some modest success packaging programs for cable, and then things took a turn for the better business-wise, but not at the personal level. Zurial seemed bound for the big time when one of the networks expressed keen interest in the pilot episode of a proposed sitcom. *Sprong & Sprang* was about two undercover cops, one neat and one messy, who are forced to work together."

"One neat and one messy? It doesn't sound very original."

"Nothing much is original in the biz," Lonnie said with a cynical smile. "It's recycle, recycle, recycle. If it worked once before, it'll work again."

I'd never heard of this particular show, but perhaps it was one never telecast in Australia. "Was *Sprong & Sprang* a hit?"

"It made it as a series, tanked, and was canceled after four episodes, but initially test audiences loved it, so the show looked set to be a big success. The promise of substantial money put Blainey and the Thorburns at each other's throats. Blainey bitterly resented that their original business arrangement split profits three ways. He demanded that either the split be amended to fifty-fifty or the Thorburns allow him to buy them out."

"I guess they didn't agree with him."

"The whole thing was headed to court when Louie and Louise conveniently died. Under the terms of the agreement, their shares of Zurial automatically went to Blainey."

"You really believe he had them killed?"

"I've no proof, but I'm sure of it," Lonnie said. "And Kylie, you need to know something more. Norris Blainey has a substantial financial interest in *Darleen Come Home.*"

CHAPTER TWELVE

I didn't see Ariana again until Monday morning. On Sunday she called me when she awoke to thank me for staying over. We had a short, friendly conversation. Neither of us mentioned the possibility of me seeing her later that day. I'd decided, after mulling over what Janette had said, that I wouldn't push it, but wait for Ariana to come to me. I did my best to ignore the grim thought that this might never happen.

I was due at Bellina Studios for a session with a voice coach at eleven, and after that I had a plethora of people to see about makeup and costumes and other esoteric things that would make perfect sense to someone like Melodie, but were pretty well a mystery to me.

Thinking that I'd be out of the office most of the day, I tidied up my in-tray, which contained mostly bills. I dutifully wrote out many checks—Lonnie's alarming stories of identity theft had frightened me away from paying through the

Internet—and trotted up to the front desk to put my envelopes in the outgoing-mail basket.

As I approached, I heard Melodie say to Harriet, "We had a *wonderful* weekend. On Friday night we even got into that hot new nightspot, Total Ennui."

Quite unashamedly, I stopped to listen.

"How did you manage that?" Harriet asked. "Bribe the guy on the door?"

"Didn't need to. Pauline was just arriving with, would you believe, Lonnie—he looked so out of place—and when she saw us, she gave the word and we were in."

"Wow," said Harriet, clearly impressed.

"Like, it was just awesome and Bruce had the *best* time. Pauline took a fancy to him and said if he could sharpen up a bit she might have a party motivator job for him. She said Aussie guys were in demand."

"I can't see Bruce as eye candy," said Harriet, "although he is good-looking."

Melodie propped her elbows on her desk and leaned forward confidentially. "Harriet, can I tell you something? Bruce is my idea of a perfect man. Brave yet sensitive." A frown darkened her brow. "Lexus thinks so too."

"A lot of heartache in these international affairs," said Harriet knowledgably. "It's not just the clash of cultures, it's the difficulty for a foreigner to live long-term in the States. Green cards are hard to get."

This was not welcome news for Melodie. "You mean Bruce can't stay?"

Harriet shook her head. "As an Australian, Bruce is officially an alien. He'll have entered the country on a tourist visa, good for a few months. He can't legally get a job and has to leave as soon as his visa runs out."

A ray of light appeared on my inner horizon. For some reason I hadn't thought of Brucie's status as a visitor to America. Brucie's plan to join Kendall & Creeling was effectively thwarted.

"What about Kylie?" Melodie asked. "Why is it OK for her to work here, when she's Australian?"

"She was born in Los Angeles. Even though she left when still a baby, she's still an American citizen."

From her expression, Melodie was brooding over the unfairness of it all. After a moment she said, "Rats! Bruce could be my one great love." Apparently the drama of the situation occurred to her, because she suddenly clasped her hands and said poignantly, "United by abiding love, yet cruelly parted by pitiless fate."

"There is a way," said Harriet. "You could marry Bruce. Then he could apply for a green card as the spouse of an American citizen."

"No!" burst involuntarily from my lips. Harriet and Melodie turned to look at me. I said hastily, "I mean, I've heard the authorities are cracking down on marriages of convenience."

Melodie scowled. "It would not be a marriage of convenience. It would be one of mutual love."

"Stone the crows," I said, "Brucie's a fast worker. He's been here only a few days, and already you're engaged."

Harriet chortled. Melodie said with dignity, "We're talking hypothetical scenarios here, Kylie."

"Besides," said Harriet cheerfully, "there's always Lexus. She might be keen enough to marry him, too."

"Wouldn't that be bigamy?" I asked. Harriet chortled some more.

"Can I do something for you?" said Melodie pointedly.

I couldn't help grinning. "Don't marry Brucie."

Melodie put up her chin. "No one's going to tell me who I can or can't marry," she announced. "If it happens to be Bruce, it's no business of yours."

"If you marry Brucie, Aunt Millie becomes your mother-in-law."

"Oh," said Melodie.

* * *

I was still grinning when I ran into Ariana on my way back to my office. We stopped outside her door.

"You're very cheerful," she said.

I told her about the unlikely—I hoped!—union of my cousin and Melodie, and how the mention of Aunt Millie as a future mother-in-law had thrown a romantic spanner into the works. "Melodie went quite ashen."

Ariana smiled, then sobered. "Kylie, about Saturday night…again, thank you for your company. And thank you for listening."

"Any time," I said. "I really mean that." Impulsively, I put a hand on her arm. "I wish I could do more."

"Just be there." Abruptly, she seemed embarrassed. "I don't know why I said that. I've no right to make demands."

"Demand away," I said lightly.

Lonnie, chomping on a pastry, came ambling along from the direction of the kitchen. "Have you brought Ariana up to speed on Blainey?" he asked me. To Ariana he said, "Dangerous SOB. Involved in suspicious deaths. Owns a piece of *Darleen Come Home*, so I told Kylie to look out for herself."

I checked my watch. Blimey, I was running out of time, and I prided myself on never being late for appointments. "Lonnie will tell you all about it, Ariana. I've got to get a move on."

On my way out I said to Melodie. "If you want me urgently, you can get me on my cell. I'll be at Bellina Studios."

Melodie's green eyes did their narrowing act. "You'll be at Bellina Studios?" she ground out. "Bellina Studios!"

"That's what I just said."

"I hope you don't break a leg."

As I knew in entertainment circles 'break a leg' was actually an oddly expressed wish for someone to have good fortune, it followed that Melodie had just expressed the hope I'd come a gutser in the acting area.

I summoned up my Pollyanna persona, practically guaranteed to sicken. "How typical of you to always be thinking of others, Melodie," I said in sugary tones. "Thank you so much. I *do* appreciate it."

"I didn't mean—"

"Oh, don't be so modest!"

I skipped out the front door in good spirits. By the time I made it across the courtyard my mood had gone into full reverse. Odds were Melodie's assessment was right. I would make a fool of myself. I had the depressing image of people all over the soundstage sniggering to themselves.

Driving along, I thought about Norris Blainey's financial interest in *Darleen Come Home*. Lonnie had explained to me how a huge concern like Bellina Studios would provide accommodation on the lot for selected independent production companies, with the understanding that Bellina would have first right of refusal for projects that seemed likely to be successful.

Blainey had invested heavily in Darleen Productions, owned by writer-director Earl Garfield. When the show became a major hit, Blainey seemed to be on a sure-fire winner. Things hadn't been so rosy recently. Ratings had been falling, and the principal cast members had been demanding renegotiated contracts for considerably more money.

I made surprisingly good time to the studios, so arrived early. This was fortunate, because there was kafuffle going on outside Bellina's main entrance. Helicopters circled overhead and a considerable crowd of onlookers waited to be entertained. People were milling around waving placards and shouting slogans. Strangely, most of them seemed to be young and very good-looking. I wondered why. Perhaps LA provided a better standard of demonstrator?

There seemed to be two distinct groups—the pro-dingo set and the pro-collie set. The cops were there in force, trying hard to keep them apart and at the same time make sure the entrance to Bellina remained open.

"Collie! Collie! Collie!" shouted one side.

"Dingo! Dingo! Dingo!" shouted the other.

Apart from the helicopters egg-beatering overhead, there were media trucks disgorging reporters and camera operators. This story was going to make the news tonight in a big way.

I found myself in a queue of cars waiting to get into Bellina Studios. Remembering that the Collie Coalition was supposed to have links to Al Qaeda, I scanned the crowd of onlookers for Secret Service types, who could be expected to be observing a demo like this. There were several who could fit the image I had of such an agent—a solemn-faced, dark-suited individual with a watchful manner. I thought they'd probably work in pairs and would talk without looking at each other, as their attention would be on the potential enemies of the country.

The head of Bellina security, Eppie Longworth, was at the boom gate with a mob of guards, who were giving each vehicle a complete going over, including using mirrors on long metal arms to check for bombs underneath each car.

"A fair bit of excitement," I said to her as I handed over my new ID card that had been in the package of stuff Howie had sent me.

Eppie used a handheld device to read the barcode on my card. "Rent-a-crowd," she said.

"Sorry?"

"Rent-a-crowd," she repeated. "Most of them are out-of-work actors. They get paid by the hour to demonstrate."

I looked back at the turmoil outside the studio gates. "Bonzer publicity," I said.

Her quick grin illuminated her face. "You'd pay millions to get this much exposure, but the media are obligingly doing it for free."

"So the media people don't realize it's a set up?"

"Oh, they know," said Eppie. "They don't care."

* * *

"No! No! *No!* Try it again: Ow-ah-ya-mate?"

"It's *mite* I said. "Mate is pronounced mite if you're speaking broad Australian."

Felicity Frobisher drew herself to her full height—not very much—and glared at me. Her masses of black, curly hair seemed to expand with her rage. "I've been a dialogue and voice coach for many years," she said in an icy tone, "and in all those years I have never, *never* had an actor correct me in this fashion."

"Sorry," I said, "but I am an Aussie, so of course I know how they speak."

Felicity Frobisher sighed dramatically. Spreading her hands, she asked the ceiling, "Why? Why me?"

I remained respectfully silent.

After gusting another sigh, she said, "Let me try to explain it simply enough for you to grasp the concept. You will be speaking an artistically modified version of the Australian accent, suitable for American ears. Otherwise, the dialogue would require explanatory subtitles running across the bottom of the screen."

"Crikey," I said, "You're not giving the audience much credit."

Felicity Frobisher folded her arms. "We're a happy little family here on the *Darleen* set. We don't make waves, we get along together. That means we don't argue with professionals who are, after all, the experts in each field, be it technical or artistic. *My* profession is particularly demanding, as it requires me to master both the technical *and* the artistic."

She paused to let this sink in, then asked, "Is it too much to ask for your cooperation?"

"Ow-ah-ya-mate?" I said.

* * *

Two hours later I was dizzy from meeting people. Through it all I concentrated on keeping straight when and where I needed to be for the shooting of my first scene the next day. If Melodie had this part, no doubt she'd be preparing by reaching deep within herself to touch the primal essence of Olive as she meets her long-lost brother, Timmy, after many years. Having no idea how to do this, I was reduced to panicking over how I'd memorize all this dialogue.

I'd found a seat in a relatively quiet corner, and was having a lash at learning a line or two, when a voice said, "And who are you?"

"Kylie Kendall," I said. "G'day."

I knew who the speaker was. Apart from the huge billboard at the entrance to Bellina Studios, over the past few days every story about Darleen and her threatened abduction had featured shots of the show's Hardestie family with Dustin Jaeger up front, his arm around Darleen. In person, Dustin seemed about twelve. He was small for his age, but he had a compact little body and an appealing face complete with endearing dimples when he smiled.

He wasn't smiling now. "The role," he said. "Who are you?"

"Olive, Jimmy's sister." I indicated the script I'd been reading. "We have a scene together."

"Dustin Jaeger will be instructing Earl to edit your lines. The emotional center of the scene is Timmy, not Olive."

I stared at the kid. Why was he referring to himself in the third person? "Aren't you Dustin Jaeger?"

He inclined his head in acknowledgement, then reached into a satchel and extracted a large headshot of himself inscribed: WITH EVERY WARM WISH FROM DUSTIN JAEGER. "Something for you to treasure," he said, handing it to me.

A harried young woman came rushing up to us. "Dustin, Earl's waiting! Darleen's on the set, and you know how she gets if she's there too long."

"That fucking dingo! You go tell the bloody wrangler that if that animal snaps at Dustin Jaeger again, he can start looking for another job."

Hopping up and down with agitation, she said, "Earl sent me to get you. Everyone's waiting!"

"Dustin Jaeger will be there after he has had a hot drink to lubricate his vocal chords."

The young woman and I watched him stroll off in a lordly fashion. "What's it with the third person?" I asked her.

She rolled her eyes. "Surely you realize Dustin's a *major star?* It's his cute little way of showing how superior he is to mere mortals like us."

"Totally up himself," I remarked.

She wasn't listening. With an expression close to terror, she squeaked, "I've got to tell Earl that Dustin isn't ready yet."

"Earl won't take it well?"

"He'll kill me! Or worse, he'll fire me."

"I'll deliver the bad news, if you like."

She stared at me with astonishment. "You will?" Then she frowned. "Why would you do that?"

"I would like a bit of a favor in return. I've been trying to get hold of Dingo O'Rourke since I got here today, but I haven't had any luck. Is there any way you can arrange for me to have a quiet word with him after this scene's finished?"

"Sure. That's easy."

"Right-oh," I said. "We have a deal. Point me in Earl Garfield's direction."

We could hear the director before we got there—a tirade of blue language delivered at a near shriek.

"Crikey," I said, "he'll blow a gasket if he isn't careful."

The set—a country kitchen—was brightly illuminated. Darleen, looking bored, was sitting beside Dingo O'Rourke. In the shadows many people silently watched as Earl Garfield marched up and down, chucking a mental. Fair dinkum, these artistic types were self-indulgent.

I stepped into the light in front of him. He halted and glared at me. "What in the hell do you want?"

"Message from Dustin. He's getting a hot drink, but will be here soon."

"That little S.O.B.!"

There was a murmur of agreement from the shadows.

Earl Garfield's face was puce. He opened his mouth, perhaps to fire me for being the bearer of bad tidings, but Dustin chose this moment to saunter onto the set, a steaming mug in one hand.

"Dustin Jaeger is ready," he said.

CHAPTER THIRTEEN

I expected people to be leaving for the day when I got back to Kendall & Creeling, but the car park was almost full. I saw with a twinge of disappointment that Ariana's BMW was missing. A gleaming black limousine sat in one of the extra spots, a stream of cigarette smoke wafting through a half-open window indicating someone was in the driver's seat.

The angst I'd caused Melodie was apparently forgotten, as she flashed a brilliant smile at me the moment I walked through the door. "Kylie, guess what! Fran's going to be honored with an award from Homeland Security!"

"Homeland Security gives awards?"

"Well they must, because Fran's getting one. The Homeland Security people are here now, inspecting her selection of disaster supplies."

Bob Verritt appeared, shaking his head. "Jeez, talk about a waste of taxpayers' money."

He folded his long, thin body into one of the new visitors' chairs—faux Spanish, thanks to Fran—and stretched his skinny legs out in front of him. "It's hard to believe, but apparently our Fran has shown superior civilian response to government catastrophe-preparedness guidelines. It seems that she's a glowing example of American get-up-and-go in the face of terrorist threats."

The black limo outside had reminded me of Phyllis Blake's run-in with the blokes at Dingo's apartment building. "How many are here from Homeland Security?"

"Two guys," said Melodie.

"Names?"

Melodie looked disconcerted, then irritated. "I didn't need to know who they were. Fran was the one they wanted."

Bob sat up. "So you didn't see any ID?"

Melodie, who'd clearly learned from Fran that attack was often the best defense, snapped, "I didn't need to. Why would they lie about being from Homeland Security?"

Bob and I looked at each other. "Why indeed?" Bob said. "Is Lonnie with them?" I asked.

"No, he's in his office. He took a call there a few minutes ago." She scowled at me. Obviously I was back in her bad books again.

"Would you get Lonnie on the phone for me, please?"

After he'd had a sneezing fit—I gathered from Lonnie's muffled curses that Julia Roberts was somewhere in his room again—I asked Lonnie if he could photograph the two Homeland Security blokes without them knowing. "Consider it done," he said.

Bob and I walked casually down the hall, discovering Fran outside the storage room detailing the disaster preparedness items she'd amassed, while Harriet and two blokes wearing dark suits and white shirts looked on admiringly.

"I had an even more comprehensive supply of sterile field dressings," Fran was saying, "but there was an unfortunate contamination problem with a cat, and then dressings were required for a genuine emergency last Friday, when my husband was badly injured outside in the parking area."

"G'day," I interrupted, putting out my hand to the closest one, a beefy bloke with thick white skin that apparently burnt easily, as his nose was peeling. He had his hair cut so short it was a reddish stubble on his skull. "I'm Kylie Kendall."

He shook hands without enthusiasm and mumbled something. "Sorry," I said, "I didn't get the name."

"Morgan."

"Mr. Morgan, g'day." I thrust my hand at the other dark suit. "Kylie Kendall. And you are…?"

He touched my fingers very briefly. "We're from Homeland Security. That's all you need to know." His voice was very soft and had a slippery, just-between-us tone. He had a long, mournful face and very deep-set eyes that seemed to be peering at the world from the back of his head.

"We're private investigators," Bob declared with his engagingly crooked grin, "so we have this need to put a name to a face."

"Unwin," whispered the bloke.

Lonnie came wandering along, a bag of jelly beans in his hand. "Want some?" he asked in a general invitation. "The black ones are the best, though I'm quite partial to the red." There were no takers.

Harriet had a quizzical, what-the-hell-is-going-on expression. She said to the blokes, "Just for the record, do you have any official identification?"

"Oh, for heaven's sake!" Fran glowered as only she could. "These gentlemen are kind enough to be considering us for official recognition for the steps we've taken to prepare for the worst." She forced a smile. "I believe mention was made of a Homeland Security Golden Plaque Award."

"I'm sure I can speak for my colleague when I say we're impressed enough to consider awarding a Platinum Plaque," murmured Unwin.

Fran's gratified expression vanished when Harriet persisted. "I'd still like to see something to prove you're who you say you are."

"It's not customary for Homeland Security to show identification," said the one who claimed to be Morgan. "It only aids terrorists who hate America because of our freedoms."

"That doesn't make sense," I said.

Morgan and Unwin began to edge away from us. "We'll be in touch," Morgan said to Fran.

"Wait! There's much more to show you." Fran gazed forlornly after Homeland Security's rapidly departing representatives, then turned savagely on us, her diminutive form trembling with rage. "Now see what you've done!"

* * *

When I compared the notes I'd taken of Phyllis Blake's detailed descriptions of the two strange men at Dingo's apartment building, it was no surprise to find Morgan and Unwin were dead ringers.

With Ariana absent—I presumed she was with Natalie—I decided that Bob, Lonnie, and I should discuss the whole matter and decide what, if anything, to do about it. Lonnie insisted that we meet in his messy office.

He was clearing bits and pieces off two chairs so Bob and I could sit down, when Julia Roberts, yawning, appeared from behind a pile of electronic equipment. I expected the usual fireworks from Lonnie, but he merely opened the door, said, "Goodbye, cat," and closed it behind her after she had leisurely exited.

"That's the way to treat Jules," I said approvingly. "Play it cool, and she'll lose interest in teasing you."

"There's something a lot more important to worry about than that damn cat," said Lonnie. "I'm sure this room is clear, as I only said hello to those guys, and then came back here to work, but I want to sweep the rest of the building for bugs."

"Would they have had any chance to plant listening devices?" Bob asked. "Fran stuck to them like glue the moment she realized a Homeland Security award was in the air."

"Trust me, the whole place could be bugged. The latest surveillance devices are so small you could be looking right at them and not notice they were there. The safest thing is to act as if every word outside this room can be overheard."

"But why would anyone bug our building?" I asked.

"Why would Homeland Security be interested in giving Fran an award?" countered Lonnie. "And were these guys even from Homeland Security?"

Lonnie had printed out several copies of the photographs of Morgan and Unwin he'd taken with one of his tiny concealed cameras. The quality was excellent. I told Bob and Lonnie how these blokes were almost certainly the ones who'd been snooping around Dingo O'Rourke's place.

While Lonnie got ready to sweep the building for hidden microphones, I went off to make sure that Melodie, Fran, and Harriet had gone, as we'd agreed it was better to keep the possibility of bugging to ourselves for the moment.

There was a crowd at the front desk. With sinking heart I saw my cousin Brucie. He'd be wanting to know all about Dingo, and would probably suggest we should have dinner together. When I got closer I became conscious of something different about him. As a rule I didn't pay much attention to men's fashions, but even I could see Brucie was wearing some really nice clothes. And his hair had the latest slightly tousled style.

I hadn't realized Quip was there, too, until I heard him say, "Since this morning I've got literary agents knocking at the door, fighting over *I, Developer.* Even had a call from a New York publisher. It was almost worthwhile being beaten up to get this level of interest."

Quip's voice was his usual light baritone, but his eyes were just slits and his face was so swollen and discolored it was difficult to believe it was really him. He was sitting on one of the new Spanish-themed chairs with Fran standing protectively by his side.

"You can thank Lonnie's blog for that interest," Harriet declared. "In some circles, he's a must-read every day. Haven't any of you seen it?"

Lonnie wrote a blog? Because of his job, of necessity he spent a lot of time on the Internet, but somehow I'd never thought of him being a blogger, freely sharing his thoughts and opinions online to a potentially huge audience.

"I'd write a blog," declared Melodie, "if only I had the time. Like, I have *a real* interesting life."

"What name does Lonnie use?" Quip asked.

Harriet made a face. "Bonnie Lonnie."

Several people groaned. I did, myself.

"Cheesy name or not," Harriet said, "Lonnie can really write effectively. Today's blog was a wonderfully satiric piece on how, inexplicably, over the years violent events occurred to individuals or companies who were unwise enough to oppose Norris Blainey in some way. Lonnie coined a term for it—the Blainey Inadvertent Kiss of Death, BIKOD for short. Quip, as the latest victim to be bikodded, was highlighted, with lots of detail about how his book is a thinly disguised expose of a certain real estate mogul's activities."

Brucie caught sight of me. With a guilty smile, he said, "Sorry, Kylie, I know I've been neglecting you, but I have no idea where the time goes. Every day is just packed with things to do."

Hallelujah! "I quite understand," I said with a faint, brave smile. "Don't give it a thought."

"Bonzer," said Brucie. "You don't mind, then?"

"Of course not. Los Angeles is an exciting city. You do have a lot to cover before your tourist visa expires."

"No worries on that score," Brucie said. "I'm working on getting a green card. I might be here for good."

Once Fran announced she was taking Quip home before he fell off the chair from exhaustion, there was a general move to leave.

"I didn't know you had a blog," I said to Lonnie when I went back to announce the coast was clear and that he could carry out his electronic sweep for bugs.

He gave me his best boyish smile. "Lots of things you don't know about me, Kylie." His grin faded. "Pauline's made a big difference to my life."

"I'm sure she has," I said diplomatically.

"I'm serious about her. In fact, I love her. Deeply."

I blinked at him. Lonnie deeply in love with Pauline Feeney? "What does she feel about you?" I inquired.

Anguish filled his chubby face. "I don't know."

"You could ask."

Lonnie shook his head. "No, I can't," he said. "I've tried, and I can't. Kylie, this might be the biggest favor I'll ever ask of you."

Crikey, I had a fair idea what was coming. I wasn't wrong.

"I must know. I can't go on with this uncertainty. Woman to woman, would you ask Pauline if she loves me?"

"Lonnie, I can't just come out with a question like that and expect her to answer it."

"*Please*, Kylie. You'll find a way. I'm dying a little each day, not knowing. You're the only person I can trust to do this."

He looked so hopefully at me, I felt myself weakening. I knew very well what it was like to love someone and not be sure if the love was returned.

"Right-oh," I said, "I'll give it a go, but don't keep badgering me about it. If an opportunity presents itself, I'll ask. If it doesn't, I won't. Fair enough?"

Lonnie nodded, sighed, then started lugging the bug detection equipment out of his room. "It's hell," he said, "this loving someone and not knowing. Hell."

* * *

Ariana came in after Lonnie had established that we were, indeed, bugged. He and Bob were in the process of finding each device and neutralizing it. I put my finger to my lips and mouthed, "We're bugged."

She raised one elegant eyebrow. I grabbed a notepad and scrawled: *Lots to tell you. I'm taking you to dinner, Musso & Frank's. Pick you up at seven. OK?*

I held my breath. This was as close as I'd ever been to taking her on a date.

Ariana gave me a long blue look, then took the pen from me and wrote: OK.

CHAPTER FOURTEEN

Musso & Frank Grill on Hollywood Boulevard first opened its doors, the menu proudly proclaimed, in 1919 and since that date had served generations of celebrities and Hollywood shakers and movers.

Ariana and I were seated in one of the many dimly lit red leather booths. The place was crowded and red-jacketed waiters with grim expressions moved without much urgency to take orders.

"They pride themselves on their surly attitude," said Ariana after one gruff waiter had taken our drink order. "It's part of the tradition."

I looked at the menu, an unpretentious white card packed with comfort food items—no complicated gourmet dishes here. "What are you going to have?" I asked, daunted by the choices available.

"Their macaroni and cheese always tempts me," Ariana said.

"Sounds good," I said. And when our brusque waiter finally delivered our food, I found it was better than good—it was addictive.

I'd already asked Ariana about Natalie. She'd been moved to a rehabilitation facility, and although her physical condition remained the same, Ariana said that she was calmer.

We discussed the bugging of our building. Lonnie had said that the devices were state-of-the-art. Tiny as a small pea, they were self-adhesive, so it was simple to unobtrusively deposit them under the edge of a desk, in the pot of an indoor plant, on the lintel above a doorway, and so on.

But who was doing the bugging, and why? It was intriguing that the same two blokes had also been snooping around Dingo's apartment building. We'd left Bob and Lonnie, armed with the photos of Morgan and Unwin, trying to establish whether or not they did work for Homeland Security. Bob was inclined to think Norris Blainey was behind the bugging and it was linked to the attack on Quip, so he was going to visit Quip at home and show him the photos in the hope he might identify the two blokes as the ones who'd bashed him.

Lonnie's cynical opinion was that Morgan and Unwin had been such clueless amateurs that they probably *did* belong to Homeland Security or some other government body.

"We can't decide on any plan of action until Bob and Lonnie find out who these guys work for," Ariana said. "So to change the subject, how was your first day on the *Darleen* set?"

Soon I had her laughing. I told her about the two opposing rent-a-crowds chanting "Dingo!" and "Collie!" at the entrance to the studios. I recounted my capitulation to Felicity Frobisher on the matter of what constituted an Aussie accent. I gave her a word-for-word of Dustin Jaeger's penchant for referring to himself in the third person, and I described how I fronted up to Earl Garfield.

I saved my conversation with Dingo O'Rourke for last. "He didn't want to talk to me, but I said I wasn't going anywhere until he did, so he finally gave in."

"I know just how he feels," said Ariana dryly.

I ignored that. "First up," I said, "you have to know Dingo is absolutely devoted to Darleen. There are three dingoes playing the part, and he says he's fond of all of them, but the dingo he loves most is the main one, and her name actually is Darleen."

In my mind's eye I could see Dingo as he talked about Darleen. His drawn face had become animated. Even his droopy mustache had seemed to perk up.

I went on to explain how he had come to believe the whole dingo napping threat by the Collie Coalition was a set-up to generate publicity for a show that was sliding in the ratings and in danger of cancellation. The idea that Darleen might be the target for abduction had first been mentioned on Internet notice boards where fans of the show exchanged messages. As rumors spread, the story reached critical mass and was broken to the general public by the media.

"Does he know who's behind the scheme?" Ariana asked.

"Earl Garfield and Norris Blainey."

"It makes sense for Blainey to be involved. He needs *Darleen Come Home* to be renewed by the network as he's in an ongoing financial crunch. Kenneth Smithson called me this morning to say rumors are circulating that Blainey is close to bankruptcy."

"Ripper! That means he won't be trying to buy our building."

"I wouldn't get too elated?" said Ariana. "Blainey's a financial Houdini. He's been close to ruin many times, but always managed to survive and prosper."

I went on with Dingo's story. "He says that until recently Blainey's only occasionally turned up at the studios, but now he's there every second day. And he's taken a big interest in the whereabouts of the dingoes. They're in their kennels at night, but during the day they're taken to different places for their exercise regimen, training sessions, and grooming. They have their own vet, and when a dingo's involved in a scene, a representative from animal welfare has to be present."

"What about on-location shoots?" Ariana asked. "Surely it'd be easier to carry out a snatch when there's no studio security to worry about."

"Dingo says all location work has been canceled. He doesn't believe it's a case of snatching Darleen, anyway. He's got the idea in his head that one of the dingoes will be killed. That's why he's taken to sleeping at the studios."

Ariana frowned. "Does it make sense to kill Darleen? She's the star of the show."

"There's three of them. As long as one dingo is left alive, the show can go on. Dingo thinks the story will be that Darleen's stunt double has been murdered in mistake for her."

"If he's so sure this is going to happen," Ariana said, "why doesn't he blow the whistle on the scheme?"

"I asked him that. He says he can't because he'll be deported and have to leave Darleen to her fate. He's here on a working visa—dingo wrangling's a rare skill, so Dingo's not displacing any American—and he's applied for a green card. He passed the background check to get the visa, but any serious investigation will turn up Aussie drug convictions under another name. Blainey dropped a hint that he knows about Dingo's criminal record, so Dingo's sure Blainey will dob him in if he blabs."

Ariana asked what Dingo had to say about the blokes Phyllis Blake had chased off.

"He said he had no idea who they were, but I didn't believe him. He clammed up then and I couldn't get another word out of him, so I left."

"Quite a full day," she said.

"You're not wrong! And to top it off, a bugging. And Lonnie."

"Lonnie? There's a problem?"

He hadn't sworn me to secrecy, but I didn't feel right revealing he'd specifically asked me to quiz Pauline about her love—or otherwise—for him, so I said, "From the way Lonnie talks, he's very serious about his relationship with Pauline Feeney. I just wonder if he's riding for a fall."

"They do seem to make an odd couple," said Ariana, "but there've been stranger combinations that have worked. Unfortunately Pauline does have a reputation for loving and leaving, and she usually dates much younger men."

"Eye candy?"

Ariana grinned. "You're getting more LA every day."

"It's just that I overheard Melodie and Harriet talking about Pauline giving Brucie a job as a party motivator, and Harriet said something about eye candy."

"To provide glitz and glamour, event coordinators like Pauline provide A-list functions with a cast of beautiful people, usually models or actors. Sometimes they're paid, sometimes they do it for free drinks and the chance to rub shoulders with celebrities."

"If you ask me, Ariana, Brucie would be way out of his depth."

"Don't be so sure. You Aussies are endlessly entertaining."

"Do I entertain you?"

Her smile faded. "You do much more," she said quietly.

We looked at each other. "Can we go?" I asked.

* * *

I was silent as I drove up the winding streets to her house. When I stopped the car outside her front door, she said, "You're coming in?"

I nodded, then got out of the car feeling giddy with desire, but terrified I'd say or do something that would destroy the fragile link between us. Surely Natalie was in Ariana's thoughts. She was in mine.

Gussie greeted us with well-mannered enthusiasm. Ariana let her outside for a run, and stood with me at the front door watching Gussie ricochet around picking up scents.

After a while, Ariana said, "She has such an uncomplicated delight in simply living."

She called Gussie inside. Closing the front door behind us, she said, "You haven't spoken a word since we left the restaurant."

I gave her a rueful smile.

"It's safer that way."

"Kylie, you can say anything to me."

"That I love you with all my heart? Can I say that?"

Ariana leaned forward and kissed me gently on the lips, then stood, pliant, within the circle of my arms. "I trust you," she said.

When we'd made love before, Ariana's cool persona had vanished in a scorching passion that set us both ablaze. Tonight was different, and even more intoxicating. She was tender, gentle, unrelenting. I was drunk with sensation. A climax that would have exploded in minutes seemed to take hours—a spring coiled tighter and tighter until it seemed the sweetest agony I had ever felt.

As she played the music of my body, I played hers. We rose together in flight, a glorious culmination that went on and on, until I believed together we would die from joy.

We shared mind and body and spirit that night. Ariana said many things, but never once that she loved me. Still, it was enough.

CHAPTER FIFTEEN

"Giles! Where the hell are you?"

It was no fun being Giles, Earl Garfield's assistant director. In fact, it was no fun being anything around this poor excuse for a human being. His balding head shining and his gray ponytail flying, he whirled around to berate some underling. Garfield was the embodiment of every arrogant, dictatorial despot portrayed in fiction. In movies behavior like his was often funny. In reality it was teeth-grindingly unpleasant.

Darleen was on the set, as in this scene she was to leap heroically through a window, sum up our perilous situation with one glance, then hurry to gnaw through the ropes that bound me to the chair. Next she was to rush to Timmy and release him from similar bondage.

She had a full entourage in attendance—Dingo O'Rourke, of course, but also a stunt trainer and his assistant, plus a groomer, who hurried forward after every take to brush Darleen's coat to gleaming perfection.

I had to admit that Darleen was the most handsome dingo I'd encountered. In the wild they were thin and scruffy, with rough coats and mean expressions. Darleen was sleek and seemed quite cheerful, although she did keep a wary eye on Earl Garfield as he stamped around swearing.

Between takes, I'd tried to strike up a conversation with Dingo, but all he said was, "Can't talk now."

Although it sounded glamorous, I was finding acting consisted of a lot of waiting around and not much action. I wished I'd brought a book to read. I'd also discovered that scenes were often shot out of order, so although Olive hadn't yet met Timmy after their decade-long separation, here she was tied up with her brother in a remote mountain cabin. I was a bit hazy about who the villains in the story were, but they had no hope against Darleen, anyway.

With Julia Roberts as an audience, I'd dutifully learnt my lines. Although no one watching was likely to call me a crash-hot actor, I thought I did a fair job under the circumstances, which were trying to say the least. First, it was fiendishly hot under the glare of the lights; second, Earl Garfield was a truly detestable creature; and third, Dustin Jaeger was deeply unhappy with the script.

We got ready for yet another take. I was tied to the chair with trick ropes which would release when Darleen rushed behind me to apparently gnaw through them. A couple of meters away, a woman in a pink smock was dabbing at a shine on Dustin's nose.

A voice shouted for quiet on the set. It was almost unnerving the way one moment people were dashing around, adjusting equipment and calling out to each other, then the next everyone was frozen in place and absolutely silent.

We had several lines of dialogue before Darleen came to our rescue. The script had Olive speaking first. "Stone the crows, Timmy!" I cried. "What will happen to us? Fair dinkum, I'm scared!"

"Is it healthy fear you feel, or primal, blind panic?" Timmy inquired.

"Cut!" screamed the director. "Jesus, Dustin, stick to the script! Your line is 'Don't be frightened. Darleen will find a way to help us.' "

Dustin looked aggrieved. "That's not how Timmy would express himself. It's not psychologically true to the existential element in his nature."

Earl Garfield made a crude suggestion as to where Timmy could put his existential element.

"Dustin's got a good vocabulary for a twelve-year-old," I said to the pink-smocked woman who had appeared with powder puff primed to eliminate any shiny spots on my face.

"Twelve? Dustin's fifteen if he's a day."

"Dinkum? He doesn't look that old."

"Small for his age, but watch out for him," she said darkly. "The little creep's got wandering hands."

I looked over at Dustin with an entirely different mindset. "The fact remains, Earl," he was saying in a superior tone, "the puerile words in your script do not in any way convey the Timmy that Dustin Jaeger knows."

"You don't know him, you little prick. If anyone does, I do. I created him."

They glowered at each other. The woman in the pink smock said to me in heartfelt tones, "It's going to be a looong day."

* * *

After an exhausting morning, we broke for lunch. I joined the stream of people heading for the Bellina Studios commissary. Outside the entrance I was astonished to see Upton and Unity in the company of a youngish bloke with a smooth tan and an intense, brooding expression.

I introduced myself to him, then said hello to the poodles, who today were wearing polished brass collars. They seemed moderately pleased to see me, although in Upton's case I noticed he cast an anxious look around, possibly checking to make sure Julia Roberts was nowhere in the vicinity.

"Pauline's inside?" I said.

"With Ursula Jaeger."

He spoke as though I should know who this was. I made an educated guess and said, "Some relative of Dustin's?"

His brooding expression vanished as he broke into a peal of laughter. "Some relative of Dustin's. That's rich!"

"Let me in on the secret. Who is she?"

"You really don't know? His dear old mom. Ursula Jaeger's the stage mother to end all stage mothers. She's a legend in this town. Uber Ursula, they call her."

Inside, the commissary was in two levels. The top one, reached by carpeted stairs, appeared to be for studio executives and other VIPs, the lower level for everyone else. I figured I was lower-level material, so I was surprised when I heard an unfamiliar voice bellowing, "Kylie Kendall! Come and join us," from the top of the stairs.

The invitation had come from a substantial sheila wearing a bright pink-and-white outfit with many flounces, ribbons, and bows, so she looked rather like a garishly wrapped parcel. Next to her at the table sat Pauline Feeney, her anorexic body clad in an iridescent green jumpsuit with a brass choker to match Upton and Unity's collars.

Pauline introduced me to Ursula Jaeger. "G'day, Ms. Jaeger," I said.

"Ursula, please! Every bloody Tom, Dick, and Harry knows me as Ursula."

She had a coarse, confident face, frizzy brown hair, and an Aussie accent, overlaid with a Yank twang. Her son Dustin's voice was much more mid-Pacific, the product of a voice coach, I was betting.

Paula said in her soft, sweet tones, "Ursula was good enough to call out to catch your attention, Kylie. I, myself, can't raise my voice. It's a physical impossibility."

"That could be bloody inconvenient," Ursula observed. "What happens if you're being attacked, raped? Are you saying you won't be able to scream?"

"I'm afraid not."

"Helluva thing! So what do you do? Whisper for help?"

"I do this." Pauline whipped out a whistle on a chain that had been concealed under her jumpsuit and blew it hard. There was no discernible sound, but frantic barking came from outside. "Beyond the range of human hearing," Pauline said. "I do hope Jason can control Upton and Unity. He's a sweet boy, but is unaccustomed to poodles."

"Give me a bull mastiff any day," declared Ursula. "Or an Irish wolfhound. Intimidation is the name of the game. Poodles are effete. They don't intimidate."

Clearly this got up Pauline's nose, but she managed a grimaced smile. "I think you'll find standard poodles are more than a match for any guard dog, Ursula. Loyal, intelligent, athletic…"

"Girly dogs," said Ursula dismissively.

Seeing trouble brewing—under Pauline's dead white makeup I detected a flush of rage—I rapidly changed the subject. "Ursula, will Dustin be joining us for lunch?"

"If he had his way, he'd love to, but I put my foot down. He's putting on weight, getting soft. I said, "No bloody lunch until you shape up. Personal trainer for you, my boy."

She eyed me. "You could do with the services of a personal trainer, yourself."

This was a bit much, as Ursula was scarcely sylph-like. "Thanks for the advice," I said, "but I'm quite happy the way I am."

"Bloody hell, are you? You're not going to hit the big time with that attitude. The entertainment industry is ruthless, you know."

"Well, actually—" I began, but Ursula was gazing past me, a pleased smile on her face.

"There's Roddy, head of Bellina Studios. He'll never forgive me if I don't drop over and have a word with him." She got to her feet and waved enthusiastically. "Yoo-hoo!"

From the expression on his face, Roddy was not looking forward to their meeting anywhere near as much as Ursula was.

"Ursula's a monster," said Pauline as we watched her trundling towards her hapless victim, "but she has her uses. We struck a deal. She gets me in to see Earl Garfield, and in return I guarantee that Dustin's invited to every A-list party Glowing Bodies coordinates for the next two months."

"But won't Garfield simply refuse to see you?"

Pauline shook her head emphatically. Her hair could have been black lacquer, as not one strand of it moved. "He can't and he won't. The ratings for *Darleen Come Home* are dropping and the vultures are circling. *Variety* is openly questioning if Garfield still has the magic touch. When the trades run stories like that it means the guy's in real trouble."

"If that's so, doesn't he lose his value as far as wrangling is concerned?"

"Not at all. Everyone likes to see a giant fall, and the harder, the better." Pauline smiled with malice as she added, "Except his ex-wives, of course. They have no interest in Earl Garfield failing."

Frankly, I couldn't see how any normal person could bring herself to marry a bloke like him. "How many wives has he had?"

"His fourth's in the process of divorcing him. The rumor is she has a generous prenuptial. Such a pity that after all that suffering, she won't get much of a pay day. She could get lucky—Garfield's resurrected dying shows before, and the best thing *Darleen* has going for it is Dustin Jaeger's popularity."

She laughed at my expression. "Sure, in person he's a self-serving little swine with an outsize ego, but in the American heartland, he's Timmy, the son they always wanted. That's why Garfield isn't going to stand up to Ursula. Oh, he'll huff and he'll puff, but in the end he'll roll over."

"Roll over enough to be wrangled?" I asked, thinking what an obnoxious guest he'd make at any function.

Pauline beamed at me confidently. "You can take it to the bank!"

"Does it matter that the bloke's likely to insult everyone he meets?"

"Honey, he can drop his pants and moon the celebrities, for all I care. Getting Earl Garfield to actually appear has long been regarded in my business as an impossibility. I'll be a legend in this town!"

I saw that Ursula Jaeger was heading back in our direction, on the way stopping at every second table to meet and greet. Conscious that I might not get another opportunity to ask Pauline about Lonnie, I said casually, "Lonnie was telling me he was at the Moonlight Reconnaissance launch on Saturday night."

"It was a stellar occasion!" Pauline enthused. "You have to understand, male fragrances are a challenge. You have to bring in the heavyweights to give the product masculine legitimacy. Athletes like Oscar, Barry, Kobe are essential, plus a smattering of older, established stars like Jack, Warren, and Tom. And trendsetters, of course—Nick, Simon, and Justin."

"Lonnie said he had a bonzer time."

She smiled indulgently. "It's a universe he's never experienced before." She waved to a waiter. "Over here! We haven't got all day."

Crikey, this was hard. I tried for a girl-sharing-confidence tone. "Lonnie's very fond of you."

"Sweet guy. Not worldly, but sweet."

"I'd hate to see him get hurt."

"Hurt? We're having fun. Haven't you heard how opposites attract?"

"So you don't see this as a long-term relationship?"

Pauline hooted. "Oh, please! With *Lonnie?*"

* * *

I left Pauline and Ursula still eating and set off for the *Darleen* soundstage. Outside the commissary Unity and Upton were snoozing in a patch of shade. The bloke's brooding expression had appreciably deepened. "Is Pauline coming soon?" he asked.

"Couldn't say, I'm afraid."

He nodded gloomily. "I knew this was too good to be true."

He seemed to want to share his pain, so I said, "What was?"

"Come with me to Bellina Studios," Pauline said. She promised to introduce me to people who'd put my acting career on the fast track. And here I am, minding her dogs."

I was fast deciding Lonnie would be much better off without Pauline Feeney in his life—not that I expected him to agree with me. On the way to the soundstage I rehearsed how I'd break the news that Pauline didn't care for him in the way he wished.

When a call came through on my cell phone, I hoped it might be Ariana. It was Quip.

"Are you home tonight?" he asked urgently.

"Yes, why?"

"It's Yancy. He's got some sensational stuff to give me. Would you let him through the gate to the alley?"

"The back gate? Why?"

"He can't be seen. Yancy says he fears for his life."

CHAPTER SIXTEEN

I was getting used to the bustle of the soundstage. I stood to one side watching as they set up the next scene to be shot, where Timmy and Olive meet for the first time. Darleen's role was simple, as she was only required to sit beside Timmy and, as we spoke our lines, look intelligently from him to me—accomplished by her trainer signaling off camera—then get up and greet me as a member of the family at the end of the scene.

Earl Garfield was nearby, considerably calmer than this morning. Perhaps he'd popped a handful of tranquillizers for lunch. He was talking to Dingo, who was frowning heavily as he listened. Darleen was on a lead, and had fallen asleep at Dingo's feet.

Seeing Dingo made me think of the two blokes who'd been at his building and had then come to Kendall & Creeling claiming to be from Homeland Security. When Bob had shown Quip the photos Lonnie had taken, Quip had said he was sure they weren't the ones who'd attacked him. Lonnie hadn't yet been successful establishing whether Unwin and Morgan were Homeland Security or not, because he'd been rebuffed with the stern admonition that it was classified information, and to release it would only give aid to America's enemies.

This official obstruction had only resulted in making Lonnie more determined and he was now hot on the trail of the limousine that I'd seen in our parking area.

A sneering voice broke into my thoughts. "Making a move from private investigation to acting, are you?"

I didn't need to look around to know it was Norris Blainey. "G'day," I said. "Fancy meeting you here."

He was dressed as I'd first seen him, in a beautifully tailored dark suit, white shirt, and red silk tie, none of which disguised the fact he was a little shrimp of a fellow with a weak chin.

"I hope you and your partner have given some serious thought to my offer?" he said.

I didn't hide my impatience. "You know perfectly well we've rejected it. You'd better get used to the fact you can't make an offer we'd accept."

Not fazed by this at all, Blainey smiled insinuatingly. "Trying to up the ante, eh? Sweetheart, you're out of your league. You're playing with the big boys, here."

I was fast getting jack of this bloke. "You're wasting your time. Kendall & Creeling's property is not for sale. Doesn't matter what you offer. Doesn't matter what you say."

His face darkened. He stepped too close to me and jabbed a forefinger in my face. "A friendly warning—I play hardball if I have to. If push comes to shove, you'll soon find yourselves begging me to buy you out."

I grabbed his wrist and forced his hand down. "Rack off," I said.

Blainey pulled himself free, his face mottled with rage. "Bitch," he snarled. "I'll have you fired from the cast."

"Jesus, Norris! Get the hell out?" bellowed Garfield. "I'm creating a show here. I don't need you interfering."

The commotion woke Darleen up. She got to her feet as, literally trembling with rage, Blainey stalked over to Earl Garfield. "Don't you *ever* speak to me that way again, you washed-up excuse for a director!" he yelled.

Darleen's lip curled, displaying sharp white teeth. Her growl was low and threatening. Dingo tightened his hold on her collar.

"Shit!" Blainey stepped back hastily. His panic subsided when he realized Dingo had Darleen under control. "That dog's a menace," he said. "She should be put down. Exterminated."

Then he turned on his heel and exited with as much dignity as he could muster.

* * *

Unhappily, the afternoon shoot resembled the morning. Dustin argued over every line, the director spewed vitriol in all directions, and the crew gritted their collective teeth.

During a break, Dingo left Darleen with her groomer and took me aside. "I can't go on this way, Kylie. Darleen senses the tension. It's affecting her work. And that bastard, Blainey, he'll make good on that threat. He'll have her killed."

I would have liked to reassure him that it was unlikely Darleen would be harmed, but Norris Blainey was clearly capable of almost anything, although I reckoned he was the type to always get someone else to do his dirty work, Quip being the perfect example of this.

His face stern with purpose, Dingo said, "If anything happens to Darleen, I'll deal with that bastard personally."

As he turned to go back to his charge, I said, "I'd be really pleased if you'd ring your parents and tell them you're OK. If nothing else, it would get Aunt Millie off my back."

Dingo grimaced. "I can't think about that now, not with Darleen and all."

"Take my cell phone number," I said, pressing one of my new business cards into his hand. "If you want to talk about it, call me."

We were about to begin the scene yet again, so Dustin and I took our positions facing each other. Darleen, looking bored, had been put at Dustin's feet. I was ready to clasp my hands to my bosom and deliver my opening line, which had been rewritten several times and was now "Leaping lizards! Timmy! Fair dinkum, is it you?" when a minor commotion occurred off set.

Darlene got to her feet and stared in the direction of the disturbance. I caught a glimpse of iridescent green, then Pauline Feeney came into full view. Beside her Jason, the brooding bloke, had Upton and Unity more or less under control. Sailing along at the rear in pink-and-white glory was Ursula Jaeger.

Garfield took one look at the poodles and bellowed, "Christ! Get those dogs out of here!"

Darlene's hair rose on her neck. For the second time that afternoon her impressive teeth came into view as a snarl vibrated in her throat. Both poodles recoiled. Upton even gave a frightened yelp.

"Gutless wonders," declared Ursula with scorn. "I told you, Pauline, they're good-for-nothing girly dogs."

Pauline gestured imperiously for Jason to remove Upton and Unity to a safer location, then turned to Earl Garfield with an ingratiating smile. "Mr. Garfield, it's so wonderful to meet you," she gushed. "I've long admired your work."

From the incensed expression on his face, the director had recognized her. "Get off the set," he hissed, "or I'll have you thrown off it."

"But—"

"Giles! Where the hell are you? Get security to escort this woman out."

Ursula pushed her not inconsiderable self in front of Pauline. "You don't mean that, Earl," she said. "Pauline Feeney's a close personal friend of mine. I'd be very unhappy if she's not treated well. Dustin would be unhappy, too."

"Yeah," said Dustin, putting in his bit.

She stood waiting, one hand on a plump hip, her mouth in a triumphant half smile. An array of emotions flowed across Earl Garfield's face, most suggesting he'd happily tear Ursula's head from her body and drop-kick it off the set.

Then the reality of the situation hit him. "Any friend of Ursula's is a friend of mine," he managed to get out in a strangled tone.

In the crew there were amazed looks all around. I reckoned no one had ever seen Garfield back down before.

Dustin took this moment to cop a feel. "Want to lose an arm?" I murmured.

His lewd grin wavered. "What?"

"I'll rip it off and beat you to death with it."

"What are you doing, Dustin?" his mother asked in a stentorian voice.

He stepped away from me. "Nothing."

I was just thinking how refreshing it was to have someone discipline the little twerp when Ursula looked me up and down and shook her head. "You can do better, Dustin. Much better."

* * *

Except for Julia Roberts, the place was empty when I got back to Kendall & Creeling. She was miffed because, as she made clear to me, I was late with dinner *again*.

"Fair crack of the whip, Jules. You almost always get your dinner on time."

She didn't look convinced, so I gave her a can of Fancy Feast chicken and liver, her favorite, as a peace offering.

Melodie had left three messages for me. I was to call Aunt Millie the moment I got in because it was "real important." The other two were mundane: confirmation for a dental checkup and a reminder from a specialist service for classic cars that

Dad's Mustang was due for an oil change. There was no urgent message from Mum, which was strange. And, although I really didn't expect it, nothing from Ariana. Maybe she'd call later.

To prepare for the rigors of a conversation with Aunt Millie, I had a shower, changed into ancient sweats, and got myself a glass of wine. Thus fortified, I dialed the international code for Oz and then her number.

"What's the latest about Dingo?" she demanded as soon as I'd said hello. "Harriet and Gert are beside themselves with worry because they still haven't heard a word from him, but someone from the government called by, asking lots of questions."

"What sort of questions?"

"Who were Dingo's friends, whether he belonged to any groups or clubs, why he wanted to go to the States—all that sort of stuff. Gert got quite short with him. Told him he had no right prying into people's private lives."

As far as I knew, Australia didn't have the equivalent of Homeland Security, but I was betting this bloke was from one of the intelligence services. "He didn't say what government department he was from or show any official identification?"

Aunt Millie snorted—her first this conversation, but I was sure not her last. "He probably did," she said, "but you know Gert and Harry. Totally scatterbrained, the two of them. No wonder Dingo's turned out nutty as a fruitcake."

"Dingo's perfectly normal," I protested.

"Normal? You call spending your life at the beck and call of a wild dog *normal?*" A mini-snort came down the line. "I don't know what's worse—the fact it's a dingo, or that its name is Darleen. Darleen!"

Belatedly I recalled that Aunt Millie's middle name happened to be Darlene. "It's spelt a different way," I said. "Your name, I mean."

"Darleen the Dingo," she muttered. "Like you'd think it was a person."

"I think Darleen is a person as far as Dingo is concerned," I said. "He's very worried about her welfare."

"A dingo's welfare! I never thought I'd see the day."

I checked the time. I had twenty-five minutes before I had to unlock the gate in the back fence for Yancy. To hurry the conversation along, I said, "Aunt Millie, I'll call the O'Rourkes if you give me their telephone number. I saw Dingo today, so I have up-to-date information."

"Better you tell me. I'll pass it on," said Aunt Millie. I could imagine the dark twist she'd put on what I told her.

"Reassure them Dingo's fine," I said, "and that he'll call them soon. Remind them that he has a stressful job. It's a lot of responsibility, caring for an animal star." I put a positive spin on a few more details of Dingo's preoccupation with Darleen, ending with, "There's been some talk of criminals snatching Darleen and holding her to ransom, so Dingo's guarding her day and night."

This got more muttering from my aunt. I'd never realized she felt so strongly about dingoes.

"Aunt Millie, I'm a bit worried about Mum. I haven't heard from her for days."

"She's got her hands full with Jack's little performance."

I sighed to myself. Mum's fiancé was, as Aunt Millie frequently pointed out, more trouble than he was worth. "What's Jack done now?"

"Taken to his bed, the nitwit. Says he can't cope, that he's having a nervous breakdown over running The Wombat's Retreat. I ask you, who deserves to indulge in a nervous breakdown over the pub? Not Jack! I said to your mother, turf him out on his ear, but she'd have none of it."

There was a pause, then she said in a less strident voice, "I can't entirely blame her. It is nice, at times, to have a man around the house."

I blinked. Could it be that Aunt Millie was getting soft? If I wasn't so pressed for time I'd ask her what she meant.

"I'll call Mum tomorrow. Now, if there's nothing else…"

"There's the matter of Brucie."

Hell's bells! No way did I want to be the one to tell Aunt Millie that Brucie was planning to stay in the States. "You haven't spoken with him?"

"Yes, Kylie, I've spoken to Brucie," Aunt Millie snapped. "I'm not at all satisfied that I know what's really going on. A mother's aware when a child is keeping something back."

I decided the safest thing was to be vague. "I haven't seen a lot of him, but he seems to be having a great time."

"Brucie mentioned a girl called Lexus. I said to him, don't put your trust in someone who's named after a vehicle, but he paid no attention. I hope I can rely on you to be straight with me, Kylie. Who is this Lexus?"

"She's a friend of Melodie's. They share an apartment."

Aunt Millie had met Melodie, and hadn't found her anywhere near serious enough about life in general. "Lives with Melodie, does she? A flibbertigibbet, I imagine."

"I've only met her a couple of times. She seems quite nice. Aunt Millie, really, I have to go."

Never one to lose the opportunity to deliver a final blow, my aunt said, "Very well, Kylie, rush off by all means. Just think about this, my girl. A child's ingratitude cuts like a knife. Brucie seems set to break my heart the way you've shattered your mother's."

I gave an exasperated sigh. "Aunt—" I broke off when I realized she had hung up.

The conversation had taken so much time I had to rush to let Yancy in. Jules looked disapproving as I galloped past her on my way to the back door of the building. I suspected that her plans for the evening included napping on my lap as I watched TV.

The gate in the back fence was secured by many metal bars and padlocks, so I went into the garage where the Mustang was parked and, without turning on the light, punched a button and opened the main door.

"Thank God! You're Kylie, right?"

He was breathing quickly as if he'd been running. His bass voice was instantly recognizable. I said, "That's me."

"I don't think I was followed," he gasped, slipping into the garage. "I left my car parked on the street half a mile away and jogged here."

After hitting the button to close the door, I turned on the light. Yancy was not tall, but he had a compact body and an intriguing, mobile face. He was so blond his hair was almost colorless. Clutched under one arm was a flat zip-up document case. He was sweating and his hands were shaking. "Can we go inside?" he said. "I don't feel safe out here."

I led the way across the yard and through the back door. "Thank God!" he exclaimed again as soon as we were inside. "Is Quip here yet?"

Yancy started violently as *Granada* loudly played. "Shit! What's that? Your cell phone?"

"Front door." I pointed to the kitchen. "Help yourself to coffee while I let Quip in."

Quip had said his eyes were still too swollen for him to drive, so he'd catch a cab. I checked the image in the security monitor to make sure it was really him before I opened the door.

Quip looked almost as furtive as Yancy. He limped in as fast as he was able, winced as he hurried to close and lock the door, then said urgently, "Yancy made it? Yes? Thank God!"

"What exactly is going on?"

"I'll explain everything in a moment." He took my arm. "Fran doesn't know I'm here. You promised not to mention anything about it, remember?"

"Where does she think you are?"

"At home in front of the TV. Tonight's Fran's yoga class."

"Fran does yoga?" This was a startling thought. I tried in vain to imagine Fran contemplating the world serenely from a lotus position.

"Has for years. Anyway, after the session she always has drinks with friends from the class. By the time she gets home I'll be back. She'll never even suspect I've left the apartment."

My expression must have shown my distaste for such deception, as Quip hurried to say, "It's for Fran's protection. The less she knows about it, the safer she is."

"Oh, bonzer," I said sarcastically. "Yet you're happy to explain everything to me. So what about *my* safety?"

"You're not my wife. They can get at me through her."

I had the strong suspicion the real reason Quip wanted Fran kept in the dark was because of Yancy. When I said this to him, Quip's battered face flushed.

"You think I'm two-timing Fran? I'd never do that. Yancy's been my main source for info on Blainey. Now he's in danger, too. So you can see why I want Fran kept completely out of it."

I wasn't totally convinced, but decided not to pursue it further. I took Quip along to the kitchen, where Yancy, clutching a mug of coffee, stood apprehensively watching the doorway. He was so nervous, sweat was running down his face and dripping off his chin. "Oh, thank God!" he exclaimed when he saw Quip. "You made it OK."

"There's an awful lot of thanking God going on," I observed.

"Yancy and I are in real danger," said Quip. "I mean, look at me. If Bruce hadn't intervened, I'd likely be crippled, if not dead."

Yancy nodded. "Norris Blainey's a murderous son of a bitch. Now that he suspects I've been feeding information to Quip, I'm at risk. The only thing to do is get out of town, go somewhere he'll never find me." He gestured to the document case on the counter. "I've brought print-outs of some of Blainey's shady property dealings. There's more where that came from. I've got it in a safe place."

"I need everything you can give me," Quip said. "You won't leave LA before passing the stuff on to me, will you?"

"Of course not. I want you to crucify the bastard."

"I had a run-in with him today," I said. They both stared at me. I added in explanation, "Blainey has a financial interest in the company making *Darleen Come Home*. I've got the part of Olive, Timmy's sister, for two episodes, so I was on the set. Blainey turned up this afternoon."

"The production company's losing money fast," said Quip. "I've got evidence Blainey's tried to unload his interest in it, but got no takers."

"I suppose you've heard about the dingo," said Yancy. "Driving here, it was all over the news."

I had a sinking feeling. Surely Norris Blainey hadn't had time to arrange her death. Then again, someone close to Darleen—the vet perhaps—could be paid enough to deliver a fatal injection. "What's happened to Darleen?" I asked.

"She's disappeared. Vanished into thin air. There's talk of a reward already."

CHAPTER SEVENTEEN

As soon as Yancy and Quip left via the back laneway—Yancy said he'd drop Quip at the nearest hotel so he could pick up a cab—I went to my room and turned on the TV to a local channel's newscast. Darleen's disappearance had not been relegated to the entertainment reporter, but was important enough to be the lead story.

There were only a few facts available, but later the police chief would be speaking to the media with further details on the eleven o'clock news. So far all that was known was that at the close of the day's shooting on *Darleen Come Home*, the star dingo had been taken to her air-conditioned run and given her evening meal. When an hour later, the kennel attendant had looked in on Darleen and her two stand-in dingoes, Darleen's run had been empty.

Also missing, the report went on to say, was dingo wrangler Douglas O'Rourke, also known as Dingo O'Rourke. As he was an Australian citizen, authorities were checking his status as a resident alien. A photo of Dingo flashed on the screen. He was scowling at the camera, his droopy mustache not hiding the grim set of his mouth. To someone who didn't know him, he looked like a villain, perfectly capable of carrying out such a heinous crime.

"A beloved dingo spirited away, who knows to what fate?" intoned the male anchor at the news desk.

His female equivalent shook her head. "Heartbreaking, Chad, heartbreaking. Many children will go to bed crying tonight."

"I feel a little like crying myself," said Chad. "There's something about an animal in peril that touches me deeply."

I changed channels. This newscast was also leading with the dingo-napping story, although the emphasis here was on how there had been rumors for some days of an extortion plot involving the snatching of Darleen. That being so, had additional steps been made to ensure her safety? Also, was the Collie Coalition merely part of a publicity campaign, or could this group actually be responsible for her abduction? And was Darleen, as star of the show, heavily insured?

These were good questions, and I was thinking about them when my cell phone rang.

"Kylie, it's me, Dingo."

"Dingo! Where are you? Have you got Darleen?"

"She's safe."

"How did you get her out of the studios?"

"It was simple. All vehicles are searched coming in, but none going out. I put Darleen on the floor behind the driver's seat, threw a rug over her, and told her to be quiet."

"You've got to bring her back before the cops catch up with you," I said.

"No way," he growled. "It's not like I've done anything wrong. Darleen's in my protective custody. If I hadn't taken her, she'd be dead by now."

"Dingo, you don't know that."

"I *do*. Yesterday, on the set, I asked Garfield for an armed guard on Darleen, twenty-four hours a day. He turned me down flat. That's when I realized he was in on the scheme to hurt her." From past experience I knew that when Dingo had his mind set on something, he was next to impossible to budge. Even so, I tried. "I can see Blainey wanting to harm Darleen—he's the kind to do that sort of thing—but why would Earl Garfield? What good does it do him to have something bad happen to the star of his show?"

There was an obstinate silence at the other end. I tried again. "I reckon Garfield was involved in a stunt to fake a kidnapping and pretend she was being held for ransom. The whole thing was aimed at getting a lot of free publicity for the show and so push up the ratings. Killing Darleen wouldn't help at all, but her triumphant rescue would."

Silence. "Dingo?" I said.

"Maybe you're right." The concession was made grudgingly. "I'll think about it. I'll call you tomorrow."

"Stop! Don't hang up."

"What? I've got to go."

"About the two odd blokes Phyllis Blake said were asking questions about you at your apartment building..."

"What about them?" he snapped impatiently.

"I'm pretty sure it's the same two who turned up here with the story that Kendall & Creeling had won an award for disaster preparedness. They gave their names, after a bit of persuasion, as Morgan and Unwin."

"So?"

"They claimed to be from the Department of Homeland Security."

Dingo swore, and before I could say anything else, he'd disconnected.

I looked at the phone in my hand. I wanted to call Ariana, not just to tell her what had happened with Dingo, but simply to hear her voice. I felt our relationship had reached a new level, but still I hesitated. Things between us were too new and fragile to put at risk.

Realizing I was hungry, as I hadn't eaten since lunch in the studio commissary, I decided to make myself a toasted cheese sandwich and a cup of tea. After that I'd think about calling Ariana.

I turned on the kitchen TV and found a cable channel running a news crawl along the bottom of the screen. Darleen's disappearance featured prominently. I learnt in quick order that: Earl Garfield, reclusive award-winning writer and director, was too upset to comment in person but had released a statement saying he was "deeply disturbed;" details of a substantial reward to be offered for Darleen's safe return would be released tomorrow; the head of security at Bellina Studios admitted she was "completely baffled" as to how Darleen had been smuggled out of the complex; the ASPCA, the Humane Society, and other animal welfare groups combined to deplore the use of an innocent animal in an apparent extortion plot; famed animal psychic Jessica de Lyons had been in extrasensory contact with Darleen and pronounced her "well, but unhappy and confused."

My cheese sandwich was history and I was pouring a second cup of tea when the phone on the wall rang. One line was switched through to handsets in the kitchen and my bedroom when the office was closed, but since I'd got a cell phone, most people I knew called me on it.

"Kylie? It's Fran. Is Quip there?"

With perfect truth, I said he wasn't. Crikey, where *was* Quip? He'd had plenty of time to get back before Fran arrived.

A frantic note surfaced in Fran's voice as she went on, "Quip can barely walk, and his face is a mess. I left him watching television. When I got home a few minutes ago, he wasn't here."

A quiver of fear touched my skin. Could Blainey have gotten to Quip and Yancy after they'd left me? Were they lying dead, tumbled in a gutter somewhere?

"Perhaps he's with a neighbor," I said, hoping against hope it would turn out to be true.

"I've been to every apartment in the building, but no one's seen him. I've called everyone I could think of I can't get hold of Mom or Ariana, so I've left them both messages to get back to me. I'm about to start calling the local hospitals."

Even if Quip were perfectly OK and off having a fine time with Yancy, as long as there was a chance he had run into Blainey's thugs again, I had to dob him in.

"Quip was here earlier this evening."

"He was! With *you?*" Her tone was deeply suspicious.

Stone the crows! Did Fran think Quip and I were having an affair? "We weren't alone. Yancy was here."

"Norris Blainey's receptionist, Yancy. I don't know his last name. He's been supplying Quip with inside information for his book."

There was a dangerous silence for a moment, then Fran said, "He? Blainey's receptionist is a male?"

"That's right."

"Start at the beginning," said Fran, her voice chillingly cold, "and tell me every last detail. Leave nothing out."

"Something could have happened to them. Perhaps we should call the police."

"Every last detail," Fran ground out. "Every last damn detail."

* * *

By the time I got Fran off the phone, I was stonkered. While I'd been talking with her, I'd imagined the worst that could have happened to Quip and Yancy. It was possible they were lying wounded in the laneway that ran behind the buildings in our block. There were no lights, and in the evening it was deserted, except for an occasional homeless person looking for somewhere to spend the night.

So, exhausted as I was, I resolved to check it out. If I didn't, I'd never rest easy. With a look of incredulity, Julia Roberts watched me arm myself with a golf club—the one I'd

inadvertently intimidated Luis with when I'd first arrived—
set my cell phone on vibrate and clip it to the waistband of
my sweats, and grab a heavy flashlight that could double as a
weapon if need be.

"Wish me luck, Jules."

"You're on your own," her expression seemed to say.

I let myself out the back door, holding it so its strong spring
didn't crash it shut with a bang. Originally you'd be locked out
once it closed and have to go around the front to get in, but
I'd had a combination lock installed, so it could be opened by
punching in the correct code.

There was a steady hum from the traffic on Sunset
Boulevard, but otherwise the night was quiet. There was
no moon, but it wasn't pitch dark because the millions of
Los Angeles lights provided a constant diffuse glow in the
sky. I opened the garage door and peered out into the lane.
Something moved, and my heart did a somersault, but it was
only some small nocturnal animal. When I'd first arrived in LA,
Lonnie had alarmed me with stories of huge rats living in palm
trees, but I persuaded myself I'd just seen a cat, and not some
horrendous rodent.

A few minutes ago when I was safely inside, searching the
laneway had seemed a perfectly reasonable step to take. Now
I was out in the darkness, it occurred to me it was actually a
pretty dumb thing to do. I reminded myself Quip or Yancy
could be bleeding to death while I dithered.

Gritting my teeth, and with the golf club at the ready, I
turned on the flashlight and, reminding myself that looking
hesitant branded one a potential victim, I strode with apparent
confidence down the lane, investigating any nook or cranny
where a body might be slumped.

I saw nothing except the occasional reflection from some
small creature's eyes. My patrol finished, I returned to the open
garage quite weak with relief. Remembering to check to make
sure no one had snuck in and was lurking behind the Mustang,

I closed the main door and let myself out into the welcome familiarity of the back yard.

I punched in the code and opened the back door. Heartwarmingly, Julia Roberts was waiting there for me.

"Back safely, Jules," I said. She twitched her whiskers to indicate her delight with the news. I was bending over to stroke her when my cell vibrated at my waist.

"Kylie? It's Janette."

"Fran got hold of you, then."

"About Quip? I'm sure he'll turn up. That's not why I called. I'm with Ariana at the hospital. She asked me to tell you that this evening Natalie had a second, massive stroke."

"Oh, Janette…"

"She's not expected to live."

"And Ariana?"

"She's devastated, of course."

I felt utterly at sea. What should I say? Do? What would help Ariana the most—my presence, or my absence?

"Janette, tell me what's best for Ariana. Should I be there at the hospital?"

Her voice gentle, she said, "Natalie's dying is between Natalie and Ariana. Do you understand?"

"I think so."

"Let her come to you, when she's ready."

How could I even imagine the grief Ariana must be feeling? My eyes filled with tears. "Tell her—" I broke off, not knowing how to continue.

"It's hard, isn't it, to find the words?" Janette's voice was warmly sympathetic. "I'm her sister, and I don't know what to say."

"Would you please tell Ariana that I'm here. That's all. Whenever, however she wants me—I'm here."

CHAPTER EIGHTEEN

Before I went to bed I called Fran to see if Quip had been found. She sounded tightly wound, but more composed than earlier. Quip still hadn't turned up, but when, after checking hospital emergency rooms, she called the police, she was told Quip had been gone for far too short a time for the cops to consider him a missing person.

"What can I do to help?" I asked.

"Nothing, thanks Kylie. Bob's here. When I called him to ask if he'd seen Quip, he said he'd come over and keep me company."

I was a little surprised. I'd never thought Bob Verritt was at all close to Fran. "Call me if I can do anything," I said. "Doesn't matter if it's the middle of the night."

I went to bed, but only dozed, as the combination of worrying about Ariana and wondering what had happened to Quip made for a night full of distressing images. I told myself sternly that Ariana and Fran had it much worse than me, but that didn't help.

On top of that I had Dingo to worry about. I wished I could discuss the situation with Ariana. Should I keep quiet? Or tell the police he'd called me? I was hazy about the law in these circumstances. Was I obstructing justice by not telling the authorities I'd spoken with Dingo?

Then there was the problem of Gert and Harry O'Rourke. His parents probably had the bad news about their son already, but should I call them to say Dingo was OK, but had admitted to me he'd taken Darleen?

My restlessness was intensely annoying to Jules, who considered the bed hers, although she kindly permitted me to share it. About two o'clock I got up and made myself hot cocoa. I was wide awake, so I decided to call my mum. It was evening in Wollegudgerie, and most of the chores of the day should be over.

"Mum, it's me, Kylie. How's Jack? Aunt Millie says he's having a nervous breakdown."

"Doc Brady says Jack's nerves are shot." She sounded quite pleased, and when I commented on this, she gave an embarrassed little laugh. "Well, I have to admit it's bonzer not to have him interfering with everything. The Wombat is running like clockwork without his help."

"Is he on the mend?" I asked. Jack had to be boss of everything, so it was hard to imagine him losing control for very long.

"Poor Jack finds it almost impossible to get out of bed, so I said to him, 'You'll be up and about when you're ready, love. Don't try to hurry things. Get up when you feel you can.'"

"Aunt Millie wasn't very sympathetic about his breakdown?" I said.

My mother tut-tutted. "She's always been down on Jack."

"And most men. But Mum, Aunt Millie said something so out of character I almost dropped the phone. It was along the lines that it could be nice to have a man around the house."

I didn't need to point out this was an extraordinary change of heart on my aunt's part. Since the death of her husband—unkind family comments suggested he'd died to escape her—Aunt Millie had maintained her highly judgmental view of people in general, but reserved her very darkest observations for the male of the species.

"That'd be because of Nigel," my mum said.

"Nigel? The name sounds vaguely familiar. Who is he?"

"Remember earlier this year, during her trip around the world, Millie did a bus tour to Bath in England? Nigel was on the tour, too, and he and Millie got on like a house on fire."

"Surely you're not telling me Aunt Millie's got a beau!"

"I wouldn't go that far, darl, but Millie acts quite girlish when she talks about Nigel coming to visit next week."

"Strewth!" I could imagine many things, but Aunt Millie girlish wasn't one of them.

"Of course he is a Pom, but even so, Millie seems quite taken with him."

"Just because Nigel's English doesn't mean he can't be a regular bloke."

My mother made a vague noise which meant she thought it unlikely, but wasn't going to argue the point.

"You'll be able to judge for yourself when you meet Nigel," I said.

"Jack thinks the bloke may be after Millie's money."

It had long been rumored in the family that Aunt Millie had considerable sums salted away, but I'd never believed it. She certainly didn't have the lifestyle of someone who was well off—she drove an old car and lived in a simple house.

"If that's the case, Mum, Nigel is going to be disappointed."

"Hmmm."

My mother was rarely non-committal, so I said, "Mum? Are you telling me that Aunt Millie is rich?"

"She's made some very smart investments over the years, that's all I'll say."

"Why doesn't she want anyone to know?"

"And have every no-hoper in the family beating a path to her door for a handout?"

Crikey! The idea that my aunt was secretly wealthy was quite a surprise.

"Kylie, you're not to mention Millie's money to anyone. I should never have told you."

"My lips are sealed."

"Enough about Millie. What have you been up to?"

"Mum, I've got a problem. It's to do with Dingo O'Rourke." I explained about Darleen's disappearance and how Dingo was the main suspect. I didn't mention Dingo's call to me, as the attempt to bug our building had made me wary of our land phones, which I reckoned could be tapped. "So what do I do about Dingo's parents?" I asked. "Maybe they know already, but should I call them and tell them what's happened?"

"Better leave it to me, darl. Gert's not likely to take it well—you know what a drama queen she is—and Harry's almost as bad."

I rang off feeling almost cheerful. I'd had a conversation with Mum during which she hadn't begged me to come home once.

* * *

After a couple of hours of fitful sleep, I got up at sunrise and went for a brisk walk around the neighborhood. I was in a jittery mood, and looked suspiciously at the few individuals I encountered at this early hour. I was oppressed by the conviction something bad was about to happen. My mum would declare this was a premonition of impending doom, but I told myself it was my natural reaction to yesterday's events. As soon as I knew Quip was OK and Dingo had returned Darleen, I'd feel better.

I forced myself to face reality—it was Natalie who haunted my thoughts. Natalie dying, or perhaps already dead. Somewhere I'd read that critically ill patients often slip away in the hours before dawn. Had that happened this morning, while I slept? Had Ariana said goodbye to Natalie for the last time?

Ariana. How would she react? Would she let me in, or would she retreat into the cool, contained persona that so effectively held everyone at arm's length? I yearned to see her, but at the same time was afraid to. How could I bear it if she'd changed towards me?

Then I was disgusted with myself. Me? It was all about me, was it? Here was I whinging about my situation when real tragedies were happening to other people. I returned from my walk vowing to get things in perspective.

I'd been given a number to call for a recorded message giving details of any changes to the day's schedule for *Darleen Come Home*. When I checked I found that the soundstage was closed down for today, out of respect for Darleen's kidnapped status, so I had time for a leisurely breakfast.

Too much had been happening for me to give a thought to Lonnie and Pauline, but when Lonnie joined me in the kitchen just as I was finishing my porridge, I realized any moment now he'd ask me if I'd had a chance to speak to Pauline about him.

Lonnie was carrying a paper bag bulging with doughnuts. "Want one?" he said, waving the bag under my nose for inspection. "There's this new doughnut shop that's opened up near me, and I figured it was my duty to support local small business."

I declined the offer. Lonnie declared, "All the more for me," and selected one smothered in chocolate.

"Did you hear about Quip?" I asked.

Lonnie nodded. "Yeah. Fran called me last night to see if Quip was with me."

"Do you know if he's turned up?"

"Haven't heard. And I didn't like to disturb her this early to ask." He took a large bite of chocolate doughnut, and a look of bliss filled his face. "Heaven," he said indistinctly.

"Lonnie, could you tell if our phones were being tapped?"

"Maybe, but if it's the government doing it, probably not, because these days the phone companies roll over and play dead the moment national security is mentioned, and it's mentioned all the time, whether it applies or not."

"What about cell phones?"

"Cell phones? No security at all. Child's play to pick up the signal. And if you're using it in a car, the transmission's transferred from cell to cell as you drive, so tracing the vehicle's route is simple."

This was not welcome news. I told Lonnie about Dingo's call to me on my cell phone. "So now you're telling me that anyone could have listened in?"

"Sure, but who'd be interested in calls you're receiving, anyway?"

"Maybe the same people who had a lash at bugging our building. Any idea yet who they are?"

"I'm on it." said Lonnie. "I traced the limousine company. Just waiting to hear from a contact in the business. I should know later this morning who those guys were working for."

I thought I'd escaped the Pauline question, but Lonnie fixed me with a soulful look. "I know you saw Pauline yesterday. Did you ask her?"

"Sort of."

"What did she say?"

I looked at his hopeful expression and my heart sank. I couldn't lie to him, but I also couldn't be cruel and tell him how Pauline had hooted scornfully at the very idea of a long-term relationship with him.

"She said you were a sweet guy, but…"

An anxious frown appeared on Lonnie's chubby face. "But what?"

"Pauline said opposites attract."

"It's true we're opposites—we could hardly be less alike. That's good, though, isn't it?"

It wouldn't be fair to let him get his hopes up, so I said, "In the short-term it is good, but not in the long-term."

He looked stricken. "Pauline said that?"

She hadn't put it in those words, so I evaded a direct lie by saying, "It's what she believes."

Lonnie's shoulders drooped. He tossed the doughnut he'd been eating onto the counter. "So she didn't say she loves me?"

"No, she didn't." I felt dreadful. I said bracingly, "Live for the moment. Seize the day."

"Pauline said that?"

"Not exactly, but she said you were having fun together. I think that's what she really meant, Lonnie—that you should enjoy your time together and let the future take care of itself."

Lonnie was obviously not going to let the subject go, so I started getting ready to provide additional tactful paraphrasings. I was saved by Bob Verritt, unshaven and rumpled, who came into the kitchen saying, "Christ, what a night."

"Quip's been found?" I asked.

"The good news is yes, Quip's turned up."

"And the bad news?"

"It looks like he's going to be charged with murder."

* * *

An anonymous phone tip at two-thirty this morning had led the police to Quip. Dazed and confused, he had stumbled out of a large self-storage complex not far from Bellina Studios. There had been blood on his clothes, and a search had revealed Yancy's body inside the half-open roller door of one of the storage units. His full name, I now discovered, was Yancy Grayson. His head had been hit with such force that his skull had broken open. A heavy steel crowbar lay beside the corpse, the hair and clotted blood on it indicating it was almost certainly the murder weapon.

Quip claimed to only hazily remember getting into Yancy's car. After that everything was a blank until he came to on the floor of the storage unit. There had been enough illumination from the security lighting outside for him to see that Yancy had been seriously hurt. He'd tried to find a pulse without success, then, feeling sick and dizzy, he'd attempted to go for help.

"There's no way Quip's a murderer," I said. "It's a set-up."

"He hasn't been charged with anything yet," said Bob, rubbing his eyes and yawning. "That's because Quip's got Sidwell Porter in his corner."

"Does Harriet know?" Lonnie asked.

"Harriet arranged it."

"I don't believe it," said Lonnie. "They haven't spoken for years."

"Who's Sidwell Porter?"

They both looked at me. "The best defense lawyer in Los Angeles," Bob said. "The go-to guy for every celebrity in trouble."

"And Harriet's estranged father," Lonnie added. "He can't cope with the fact she's gay, and worse, that she is openly living in a lesbian relationship."

"Fran woke Harriet up and begged her to approach her father," Bob said. "I've never heard Fran so close to hysterical. Harriet finally said she would, although she told Fran it was unlikely he'd agree. Seems she was wrong—Harriet called back to say he'd represent Quip."

"Why the change of heart?" Lonnie said. "Porter's daughter hasn't stopped being gay."

Bob shrugged. "Maybe the fact that she's about to make him a grandfather. Harriet's his only chance of that, as she's his only child."

Lonnie nodded moodily. "I'll never be a grandfather," he said.

Bob's long, thin face split with a grin. "You're putting the cart before the horse. You have to be a father first."

"That too," said Lonnie. "I won't be a father, either." He picked up the bag of remaining doughnuts and handed it to Bob. "Want these? I've lost my appetite."

Head down, he shuffled out of the kitchen. Looking at Lonnie's retreating figure, Bob said, "What's the matter with him?"

I wasn't going to betray a confidence, so I said, "Search me."

Bob tried a doughnut. "Hey, these are good. Want one?"

"No thanks. Bob, can I ask you something?"

He laughed. "Nothing's ever stopped you before."

"It was so nice of you to stay all night with Fran."

"I wasn't alone. Fran's mom turned up just after twelve, so there were two of us rallying around."

"Still, it was bonzer of you."

He gave me a shrewd look. "You're thinking Fran and I don't always see eye to eye, aren't you?"

"It did cross my mind."

His expression bleak, Bob said, "I've experienced what Fran went through last night. I know what it's like to be frantic with worry, and what a comfort it is when someone's there to share the waiting. And at least Quip's alive."

"Who was it?"

"My sister. Fifteen years ago. She was going to have dinner with me. She left work, got in her car, and simply vanished. There was no suggestion she'd disappeared voluntarily. Kerrie was in good spirits. She'd just got the promotion she'd been working hard to achieve, and was engaged to someone she adored."

I was chilled by the forlorn sorrow on his face. "She was never found?"

"Never. It was if she'd never existed."

Lonnie reappeared, even more doleful. "You'll never believe it, but those two clueless guys, Morgan and Unwin, *are* with Homeland Security." He paused, then added dramatically, "And they're investigating Kendall & Creeling as a terrorist organization."

CHAPTER NINETEEN

It was mid-morning, and Melodie, Harriet, Lonnie, and I were holding down the fort. Bob had gone home to snatch a few hours sleep, and Fran, of course, was occupied with Quip's dire situation as chief suspect in a violent murder. I hadn't heard from Ariana and had decided not to try to contact her, but to let her decide when she wanted to talk with me.

Murders were not a rare occurrence in Los Angeles, so it took something extra to get the media's concentrated attention. Unhappily, Yancy's death had two media bonus points. First, he had a connection to real estate mogul Norris Blainey, and second, the chief suspect was not only involved in the entertainment industry, always a point of keen interest in this city, but also happened to be writing a novel skewering a thinly disguised Blainey. The fact that Quip was married to the daughter of the well-known artist Janette—like Cher, Janette only used her first name—gave the story an added boost.

So Yancy's murder got the full media overkill, and Darleen's snatching became very much yesterday's news, even though a quarter-million-dollar reward had been offered, and the dingo-snatcher had been named definitively as Douglas "Dingo" O'Rourke.

Quip's connection to Kendall & Creeling through Fran had been discovered, and the phone rang constantly with requests for "background" on Fran and Quip, a camera crew appeared in the street outside our building, and we were forced to put a sign on the front door stating firmly that there would be absolutely no interviews granted.

From the time she'd arrived Melodie had scarcely left the front desk, as along with the media, the receptionist network was fairly burning up the wires. She was also fielding calls from curious Kendall & Creeling clients as well as friends of Fran and Quip's.

To sustain her I brought Melodie a mug of coffee—decaff, low-fat milk, artificial sweetener—and a carton of strawberry yogurt—low-fat, artificial sweetener, artificial flavoring. Yerks!

Melodie finished a call and looked up at me, face full of flinty resolution. "We have lost one of our own," she said. "Murdered."

Crikey! It was like the receptionists were a secret guild. "It's a blow, I'm sure," I said.

"Don't mess with us."

Puzzled, I asked, "How am I messing with you?"

"Oh, Kylie, not *you*. I mean whoever killed Yancy. Everyone's terribly upset and determined to do something about it."

Obviously I was overtired, because I immediately had a vision of thousands of receptionists arming themselves with Sherlock Holmes deerstalker hats and large magnifying glasses and sallying forth to find Yancy's murderer.

Repressing an entirely inappropriate grin, I said, "What something could they do?"

Melodie shook her head. "You've got no idea, have you? No idea at all."

"Apparently not."

"Nothing happens in this town that we don't eventually find out about."

Melodie stated this with justifiable pride. Even I, in the relatively short time I'd been in LA, had seen the receptionist network's almost alarming ability to collect and disseminate confidential information.

The phone rang. "Good morning, Kendall & Creeling—oh, Bruce, hi! Yes, she's right next to me. Hold on."

I'd completely forgotten about Brucie. I wondered why he wasn't here, enjoying all the media attention that was raining down on us. Reminding myself to get his name straight, I said, "G'day, Bruce."

"Morning, Kylie. In case you're wondering where I am, I'm with Quip and Fran. Someone's got to keep the bloody reporters at bay."

"How are they coping?"

"Not too good, but at least Sid, the lawyer they've got, is a top bloke. He says no worries, he'll get Quip off. Did you know he was Harriet's dad?"

"I found out this morning." I didn't want to get into a long conversation with him, so I said, "I'll let you get back to guarding Fran and Quip from the media."

"Hang on a mo. I need to ask you something about my mum. Have you heard about this Nigel who's coming to visit her?"

I said my mother had mentioned the name.

"I'm not too happy about it," said Brucie. "He's coming all the way from England to Wollegudgerie, just to drop in on Mum. And I can tell from the way she talks about the bloke that she's a bit soft on him. And he's a total stranger." He added in dark tones, "Who knows what he's up to?"

"What do you think he's up to?"

"I reckon he's after Mum's money. She doesn't flaunt it, but she's got quite a bit salted away."

"What if Nigel's visiting because he likes her? Maybe there's something romantic between them."

"Aaagh!"

"You'd be opposed?" I inquired.

"Blood oath I'd be opposed! I'm not going to stand by and let my mother be taken advantage of." After a couple of muffled curses, he said, "Gotta go. I'll ring Mum right now and see what the hell is going on."

"Kylie," said Melodie as I put down the phone, "do you know what's wrong with Ariana?"

"Why would something be wrong?" I asked, stalling for time.

"She's been out of the office loads more than usual, and Bob's been looking after her clients for her. Like, is she sick?"

"Ariana isn't sick."

Ariana was an intensely private person, so she would never have mentioned Natalie to Melodie. Of course Fran, being Ariana's niece, must be aware of Natalie's existence, but evidently she hadn't said anything to Melodie.

An inspiration struck me. "Ariana's worried about Norris Blainey and his plans for the neighborhood."

Melodie's face cleared. "That must be it." The phone rang. "Good morning—oh, Laurel, hi. Have you heard anything more?" She listened intently. "Try Riley, she knows her well… Like, get back to me ASAP. Bye."

"There you go," she said to me with a triumphant note in her voice, "I told you no one should mess with us."

"Your network's found out something?"

"Maybe. That's all I'll say." She looked past me. "Hi, Ariana."

"Good morning, Melodie." Ariana closed the front door behind her. "My office?" she said to me.

"Right-oh."

I followed her down the hallway. She moved as if unutterably weary. Inside her office, she looked at me with austere calm.

"It's over. Natalie died this morning." The blue of her eyes was drowned in sudden tears. "It was a relief."

I put my hand on her shoulder. "You must be so tired."

She nodded slowly. "I hope you understand. I need to be alone."

"I understand."

I did. If I had lost Ariana, no other person would be able to share my journey from sharp grief to final muted acceptance.

She put her hand over mine. "Thank you."

There was a knock at the door. Ariana stepped away from me to open it.

"Somewhat of an emergency," said Lonnie. "Has Kylie told you Homeland Security is investigating us as a potential terrorist cell?"

Tired though she was, Ariana snapped to attention. "We're a terrorist cell? You've got to be kidding."

"It's Fran made them suspicious in the first place, and now that Quip's the suspect in a murder, they're even more revved up."

Ariana went behind her desk and sat down. Waving us to chairs, she said, "I haven't discussed it with you, Kylie, but I'm sure you'll agree that we should devote every resource to helping Quip clear his name."

"That goes without saying."

Ariana rubbed her eyes, then straightened her shoulders. She was so pale her eyes burned in her face. "We need a meeting of everyone concerned, to make sure we're all on the same page. I suggest nine tomorrow morning."

"Do you want me to arrange it?" I asked.

"Would you? Thanks." She turned her attention to Lonnie. "OK, start at the beginning, Lonnie. What's your source for this information about Homeland Security?"

"First off, the guys that bugged our building have been using a limo service to get around. Can you imagine? A limo? Our tax dollars at work!"

"Shocking," said Ariana dryly.

Lonnie went on to say how he'd traced them through the limo company and discovered the Department of Homeland Security was picking up the tab. He'd also posted the photos of Morgan and Unwin widely on the Internet and received several positive responses. The most interesting had been from someone who headed a clandestine group sarcastically titled Homeland Insecurity, who confirmed that Morgan and Unwin were the agents' real monikers—Richard Morgan and Allan Unwin to be precise.

"The guy running the group calls himself Milt, but that probably isn't his name," said Lonnie, "Homeland Insecurity's mission is to expose Homeland Security's waste of taxpayers' dollars, attacks on civil liberties, and general ineptitude. Milt has several people inside DHS who he calls true patriots, devoted to exposing the astonishing inability of a department funded with billions of dollars to accomplish an even halfway decent job."

"What about Fran?" I asked. "Did this Milt bloke tell you why she came under suspicion?"

"Two words: disaster supplies," Lonnie said. "If Fran had been content to limit herself to the preparedness items that Homeland Security recommends, none of this would have happened. But no! She had to go overboard."

"I'm betting it was the full-body biohazard suits that set off a red alarm," I said.

"That and the military food rations, battleground medical kits, and drugs for smallpox, anthrax, and so on."

"Not to mention the forty gallons of water," I added.

"I can see why Fran's concept of disaster supplies might catch official attention," said Ariana, "but any background check will show there's no one at Kendall & Creeling who could conceivably be a terrorist."

"Ah," said Lonnie, waggling a forefinger, "that's precisely why that bunch of paranoid incompetents think we *are* likely terrorists—our cover's so good. Milt explained how they love to connect the dots and come up with conspiracy theories that would put Hollywood to shame."

"And how does Quip being a murder suspect play into this?" Ariana asked.

"That's the best part." Lonnie beamed at us. His dimples and lock of hair falling over one eye made him look like a mischievous kid. "The murder victim worked for Norris Blainey." He paused for a dramatic beat—honestly, Lonnie was as bad as Melodie at times—then said, "And Norris Blainey has been an informant for Homeland Security for some time. You can imagine when his name came up and there was a connection with Kendall & Creeling, a suspected terrorist cell, it caused quite a stir."

"Much dot-connecting," I remarked.

"Who's Blainey been targeting with the tips he's been giving Homeland Security?" Ariana asked.

"Business competitors mainly. One of Blainey's favorite claims is to suggest the person he's named is laundering money for terrorist organizations."

"Doesn't he get discredited," I said, "when none of his tips are dinky-di?"

"That's where Blainey's clever," said Lonnie. "He's in a good position to hear whispers of larceny and worse in the financial world, so some of his accusations do turn out to be true."

"That gives him credibility," said Ariana.

Lonnie grinned at me. "Speaking of connecting the dots, there must have been some excitement when some bright spark in Homeland Security realized Douglas 'Dingo' O'Rourke was your cousin."

"Blainey dobbed Dingo in to Homeland Security?"

Lonnie nodded. "He told them he thought O'Rourke should be treated as 'a person of interest,' and you know what that means."

"It means your life's not your own anymore," remarked Ariana acerbically.

Lonnie chimed in with, "A magnifying glass on anything and everything you've done or said. No stone left unturned."

"Crikey," I said, "if that's the case, what are we, being suspected terrorists?"

Lonnie made a face. "Persons of extreme, intense, and acute interest."

Wouldn't it rot your socks?

CHAPTER TWENTY

On Thursday I wasn't required at the studios until the afternoon, so there was no problem about attending the meeting Ariana had called. Bob and I had carried extra chairs into Ariana's office and by nine o'clock we were all seated. Ariana was behind her desk, the rest of us arranged in a semicircle facing her. The phones were still switched through to the answering service we used after hours, so Melodie was present, as were Bob, Lonnie, and Harriet. Quip, looking like death warmed up, was slumped in one of Ariana's comfortable black leather armchairs. Fran, looking not much better, was next to him.

On the surface Ariana seemed her usual cool, reserved self, although there was something brittle about her manner, as if she maintained a façade by sheer force of will.

"Before we begin," she said, "you all now know that the local office of the Department of Homeland Security has seen fit to designate Kendall & Creeling a possible terrorist cell."

Melodie glared at Fran. "Thanks, Fran," she said with heavy sarcasm. "Thanks very much."

A flash of her customary combativeness animated Fran's face. "Don't blame me for doing what any good citizen should do for disaster preparedness. You'd be the first in line, Melodie, if smallpox happened to be ravaging your body, covering your skin with bursting, toxic pustules."

This gave Melodie a bit of a jolt. She looked down at herself as though expecting to see signs of smallpox popping out all over.

I said, "It's hardly Fran's fault if these government galahs leap to ridiculous conclusions on the flimsiest of evidence."

Fran stared at me, clearly astonished to find me defending her. I gave her a little grin. "You can pay me later."

"The only way to deal with such accusations," said Ariana, "is to make a several-pronged counter-attack. Bob has contacts high up in the FBI and CIA, and he's made them aware of these totally unwarranted allegations."

I glanced across at Bob, his skinny frame folded awkwardly into his chair. I'd taken his pleasant, uncomplicated surface personality as being all there was to him. I was realizing belatedly I didn't really know much about the real Bob at all.

Ariana went on, "For my part, I've spoken with Senator Lawry, who is not only our Federal representative, but also a long-time critic of government intrusions into citizens' lives. I'm hopeful he'll pull some strings on our behalf. Finally, Lonnie is in the process of spreading details of our persecution, as he rightly calls it, across the Internet."

"What about the media?" Harriet asked. "You know how they love 'it happened to them and horror! it could happen to you' stories."

"That's our next move," said Ariana, "if we get nowhere with the head of the Los Angeles DHS. He's indicated he'll be happy to discuss the matter. I'm waiting for a firm appointment. Now let's move on to the much more important subject of Quip."

In a husky, halting voice, Quip recounted what he remembered of Tuesday night and Wednesday morning. When he and Yancy had left me they'd walked along the lane and onto a side street where Yancy had parked his car. Yancy had been literally shaking, Quip said, although no one seemed to be watching them and they saw nothing suspicious.

Once in the car, Yancy had blurted out that he was so terrified of what Blainey might do to him that he'd made the decision to leave town that very evening. If Quip wanted all the material Yancy had taken from Blainey's office, he would have to come with him to the self-storage complex where Yancy had the documents safely under lock and key.

"Yancy had a hip flask of whiskey," said Quip. "Before he started the car he took a swig from it—at least I thought he did—and handed it to me. By this time I was feeling every bruise and cut from the beating I'd taken, so I took a couple of good mouthfuls. Yancy started driving, and I remember he kept looking over at me. After a few minutes, I began to feel dizzy, and then, like they say in books, everything went black."

"Date rape drug," said Fran bitterly. "Rohypnol, GHB, something like that. Leads to partial amnesia—that's why Quip can't remember much of what happened."

Quip described his total confusion when he regained consciousness inside the storage unit to discover Yancy's body on the floor beside him. He couldn't find a light switch, but the roller door was half open, so Quip could see that Yancy's head had been dealt several savage blows. In the dim light, he'd missed seeing the crowbar which had now been proved to be the murder weapon. Quip had stumbled out into the street to find help and had found himself blinking in the glare of police lights.

"They made me empty my pockets. I still had my wallet, credit cards and money untouched, but my cell phone was gone and when we went back to the storage unit, so was the document case Kylie saw Yancy give me earlier."

"I reckon the hip flask had disappeared, too," I said.

Quip nodded. "Of course it had. I was set up for Yancy's murder."

"Bad apple," Melodie said dejectedly. Everyone looked at her.

"Who is the bad apple?" Fran asked with a dangerous glint in her eye.

"Not Quip," said Melodie. She sighed gustily. "You think you know someone, speak with him practically every second day, and you never suspect he's a bad apple."

"Enough with the bad apples!" Fran snapped. "If you're talking about Yancy Grayson, say so."

"Melodie, tell them what you know," said Ariana. Her voice had none of its normal authority. I looked over at her and our glances locked.

I didn't say "Are you all right?" aloud, but the love and concern I felt must have been obvious to her, because she nodded slightly and gave me a faint smile.

This was Melodie's limelight moment. I'd bet a motza she'd spent ages rehearsing for this performance. She scanned the room, apparently to assure herself that we were all paying attention, took a deep breath, and began, "Yancy is—was—the principal receptionist at Norris Blainey's offices. Because of the volume of important calls coming through the switch, he had a designated relief receptionist, so that there was always a trained professional to answer the phone." She paused to reflect. "You know, not enough companies understand the impact of the first voice a client hears."

"Get on with it?" Fran snarled between clenched teeth.

"I am getting on with it," said Melodie with dignity.

Lonnie groaned. "I'm hungry. Is this going to take all morning?"

"As I was saying before I was interrupted"—Melodie broke off the glower at Lonnie—"Yancy had Merle, a relief receptionist. She's fairly new at the game, but she has promise."

"Steady, Fran?" I said. "Melodie will get to the point any day now."

Melodie ignored this and went on, "As often happens when professionals sharing vital responsibilities are thrown together, Yancy and Merle became more than colleagues, they were friends and confidants. Merle had nothing much to confide—she's young and leads a simple life."

The real Melodie broke through when she added, her green eyes wide, "But Yancy had lots to tell her and it was *real* interesting…"

Quip put his head in his hands. Ariana said, "Cut to the chase, Melodie. Now."

"Yancy told Merle that he'd been passing info about Blainey to Quip for his tell-all book. Yancy did it because he wanted a career in show business and he was hoping Quip could open doors for him." She shook her head. "I could tell, even on the phone, that Yancy didn't have that glow, that star quality. It's real tragic, really."

At this point a concentrated group glare speeded up Melodie's delivery. "OK, this is how it went down. A few days ago Norris Blainey found out what Yancy was doing. Blainey went off his head. He said he'd have Yancy's knees smashed, his fingers broken, and his face slashed if he didn't follow instructions exactly. Yancy had to set up a meeting with Quip here, on Tuesday night, and make sure someone witnessed it. Then he had to persuade Quip to go to a certain unit in the self-storage place by telling him he had much more stuff on Blainey there."

"This guy believed in fairy tales, did he?" Bob said. "He thought Blainey would simply let him go?"

"That's what Yancy told Merle."

"And what did this Yancy think would happen to Quip?" Fran demanded.

"He didn't know."

"It's a good thing he's dead—I would have killed him myself," Fran muttered.

"If she hasn't already, this Merle has to tell her story to the cops," Lonnie said.

"Merle won't," said Melodie. "She's terrified of Blainey. When the police interviewed people in the office, Merle told them she didn't know anything. She trusts other receptionists, but no one else."

"Can't blame her," said Harriet. "She's seen what happened to Yancy."

"I certainly *can* blame her," snapped Fran, leaping to her feet. Like a pocket-sized Amazon queen, she bounced on her toes, ready for hand-to-hand combat. "Lead me to this Merle. I'll rip the truth out of her."

Quip reached up to put his hand on Fran's arm. "Sweetheart, calm down. Harriet's father should interview her. If the worst happens and I'm charged with murder and there's a court case, she'd be a witness for the defense. *My* defense."

Fran's militant stance deflated. I was surprised and almost embarrassed to see Fran bend her head and kiss his fingers. Fran never was demonstrative that way.

Before the meeting broke up, Ariana allocated tasks. Ariana herself would liaise with her contacts high up in the LAPD and Bob would investigate Blainey's movements on Tuesday and Wednesday to establish if he had an alibi for the time of the murder—estimated as somewhere between ten and twelve on Tuesday evening. Harriet, whose relationship with her father was still very tentative, would monitor developments in Quip's defense through her father's personal assistant. Melodie was to report any further information her network could glean. And Lonnie would carry out an in-depth background search of Blainey's staff, concentrating particularly on relief receptionist, Merle.

"What about me?" I said. "What do I do?"

"Kylie, it's not necessary for you to do anything," said Bob with a grin. "It's quite extraordinary, but you're what I call an event magnet—things just seem to happen to you."

For some reason this amused everyone. Even Ariana smiled.

"Is that a compliment, Bob?" I asked.

"Absolutely," said Bob, laughing. "Life before you was quite boring, in retrospect."

Ariana said to me, "You've got your hands full with Dingo O'Rourke and the missing dingo. When that's resolved, you can get involved with Quip's case."

The meeting over, Lonnie helped me carry chairs back to respective offices. "About Pauline..." he said.

Uh-oh! There was no way I was going raise the subject of Lonnie with her again.

"Thing is, Kylie, I've decided to win her hand."

"I beg your pardon?"

"I'm rising to the challenge, not giving up. I'm going to woo Pauline, sweep her off her feet, show her the inner, romantic me."

"Blimey," I said, "do you think she's ready for this?"

Lonnie's face was flooded with eager enthusiasm. "I'll be the love train coming down the tracks. Pauline won't know what hit her."

I was afraid he was right.

* * *

I was in my office learning my lines for the afternoon shoot when Dingo called on my cell phone. Lonnie had said the cell wasn't secure, but I didn't want to scare Dingo off, so I didn't mention this.

"Jesus, Kylie," he said, "I'm screwed. Blainey's hung me out to dry. You saw the reward for Darleen is a quarter of a million?"

"It was on the news. And so were you, Dingo."

"That bastard, Blainey! He set up the scheme in the first place, but now he's out to get me."

Blainey had engineered Darleen's disappearance? "So Darleen wasn't in any danger at all?" I said.

"Of course she was! That's why I took her."

"You've lost me, Dingo."

He gave an exasperated sigh. "It's too bloody complicated to give you all the details, but Blainey had this scheme to get the maximum publicity in order to bump up the ratings of the show. The story would be that Darleen had been kidnapped and held for ransom and that I, being a fair dinkum Aussie from the Outback, would use my ancient tracking skills to find Darleen and rescue her."

"So what went wrong?"

"It was me put Darleen in harm's way. I had something on Blainey, and when I tried to collect, he turned on me."

"You tried to blackmail Norris Blainey?"

"The bastard didn't take it well," said Dingo. "And then he decided to punish me by having Darleen killed."

"He also sooled the Homeland Security blokes onto you. What was that about?"

"There's a lot you don't know. I've got to have insurance, or I'm dead meat. I mean it, Kylie. Blainey wants to get rid of me. Permanently."

"Go to the police."

"I can't. I'm up to my neck in it. You're working with that high-powered PI, what's her name? Creeling? Well, I want to hire her."

It was stupid of me, but I felt quite hurt. "You were sort of my case, Dingo."

"No offense, Kylie, but you're a beginner at the private eye racket. I need someone who knows what they're doing."

I told him I'd speak to Ariana, but at the moment she was fully engaged with Quip's case.

"Then she'll want to see me," he said. "I know all about that, too."

"You do?"

Perhaps there was a note of doubt in my voice, because Dingo snapped, "Bloody hell, I *do*. I never went through with it, I swear, but I taped Blainey offering me a cool two hundred thousand to kill Yancy Grayson."

CHAPTER TWENTY-ONE

Ariana, Bob, and I discussed the Dingo situation. Dingo rightly feared Blainey, who knew he was in possession of an audio of Blainey recruiting him to murder Yancy. We agreed it was vital for Quip's case to have Dingo tell his story to the police. It was going to be difficult to persuade him to, but the first step was to get together face-to-face.

I was worried about Ariana, who seemed strained to the breaking point. "Why not leave it all to Bob and me," I said. "When Dingo calls back this evening to organize how and when he'll meet you, I'll say you're not available and that you've recommended Bob to take your place."

"We may all be in government detention by then," said Ariana with a wry quirk to her mouth. "I've just been told that the LA director of the Department of Homeland Security—an individual so cloak-and-dagger that I wasn't permitted to learn his name—will be paying us a visit here at seven this evening after the staff have gone. You and I, Kylie, as co-owners of the business, are expected to be present, and I asked that Bob, being our senior investigator, be included too."

"Yerks! Is there really a chance we'll be arrested?"

"Anything's possible," said Ariana, "but I think it unlikely."

"I'd better leave out extra food for Julia Roberts, just in case." We arranged to meet in Ariana's office at six-thirty, then Ariana went home, Bob went back to work, and I set off for Bellina Studios.

I was getting the hang of this TV acting, which essentially consisted of copious amounts of standing around, and then a few intense minutes when the cameras were on me. Things were greatly helped by the fact the scene being shot didn't require Dustin as Timmy, so everything went quite smoothly. By four-thirty I was on my way back to Kendall & Creeling.

The traffic was heavy, so everyone was leaving by the time I got back. Melodie was getting into her jazzy red sports car as I parked my subdued dark-gray Toyota. Seeing me, she got out and came over.

"Kylie, can I ask you something?"

"Ask and ye shall receive."

She frowned at me. "What?"

"What can I do for you?"

"Bruce is real worried about his mom. He thinks this English guy is only after her money. I was wondering, does she live on a big cattle ranch?"

Aunt Millie had a simple little house in Wollegudgerie, by no stretch of the imagination a cattle station. "Did Brucie tell you that?"

"No, but Lexus and I were watching *The Thorn Birds* the other night, you know, that old series with Richard Chamberlain as the priest who falls in love? So romantic! Anyway, there was this humongous Aussie ranch, and Lexus said Bruce's mom lived somewhere just like that."

"I hate to disillusion Lexus, but it isn't true. Brucie's mum lives in a perfectly nice house in a country town."

"Oh, good," said Melodie. She leaned forward to say confidentially, "Lexus thinks Bruce comes from a rich family. I think that's why she's so interested in him. She'll be so disappointed."

Melodie trotted cheerfully back to her car and I went inside, musing over what to wear to meet the nameless national security bloke. Julia Roberts was waiting for me at the front door.

"Jules," I said, "you've got good taste. What do you recommend I wear to meet a high official in Homeland Security? Do you think something really dressy?"

Julia Roberts slanted her ears quizzically. "You're absolutely right," I said, "plain and simple is better for these government types."

I changed into black jeans and a green silk shirt and made myself a cup of tea. In case this meeting took some time, I served Julia Roberts her dinner early.

Around six-fifteen there was a commotion outside. I put my head out the front door. The place was crawling with limousines and people in dark suits. "Stone the crows," I said to Jules, who'd been attracted by the noise, "it's like the president's arriving."

The top honcho of the DHS turned out to be a disappointment. I was expecting someone commanding, with a military bearing, eagle eyes surveying the lay of the land, and all that stuff, but he was an insignificant man with a soft face and the hint of a pot belly. Accompanying him were Morgan and Unwin. "G'day," I said to them. "Ripper to see you again, even if you are a bit early."

"Keeps people off balance," whispered Unwin in his slippery voice. There wasn't a hint of humor in his long, grayish face. He looked slight beside Morgan's thick-necked wrestler's build.

To be polite, I said, "G'day," to the top honcho, too. "I'm Kylie Kendall."

"I'm afraid I can't tell you my name or title for national security reasons." He had a bossy manner and a slight lisp.

"Right-oh," I said.

Ariana and Bob arrived as I was ushering the three of them into the reception area. Bob was cheery, Ariana distant. Morgan and Unwin went along to check Ariana's office for dangerous devices while the rest of us waited by Melodie's desk. The head bloke stood silent, gazing at nothing in particular, so Ariana, Bob, and I were silent too, although I caught Bob's eye and grinned. He gave me a warning, don't-cause-waves look in return.

Morgan and Unwin came back with the all clear, so we trooped down the hall to Ariana's stark black-and-white room.

Once Ariana, Bob, and I were seated and Morgan had taken position guarding the door and Unwin the window, the head honcho began to walk up and down, looking self-important. "Many have been the representations made on your behalf," he announced, "and these have persuaded us that you are not, and never have been a terrorist organization."

He paused for reactions of joy or relief. Ariana said coolly, "We would appreciate some explanation for this baseless accusation."

"Indeed." He cleared his throat and continued officiously, "We regret that analysts in the Department unfortunately mistook the admirable diligence of one of your employees in the realm of disaster preparation as an indication of possible terrorist activities. We acknowledge that this person is, in actuality, a deeply concerned citizen."

"How about these two clowns here trying to bug our building?" Bob asked.

Everyone looked at the two clowns. Morgan ran a hand over the red stubble on his skull, Unwin stared morosely at the floor.

Irritation washed over the head bloke's face. "We also apologize for the attempt to plant listening devices in your premises. Again, this was a misguided but genuine effort to ensure the safety of our great nation. I assure you that this will not occur again."

He paused, then added, "Unless, of course, a terrorist should enter your employ in the future."

"Well, *that's* likely," I said.

Another pause. I had an almost irresistible desire to giggle, but a warning glance from Bob calmed me down.

Then the bloke was off again. "Another matter of extreme importance has come to our attention. Connecting the requisite dots convinces us that there is a deep-seated conspiracy with Norris Blainey at the centre. Unaccountably, Mr. Blainey has been a trusted informant to DHS"—he glared meaningfully at Morgan and Unwin—"while carrying out activities that are little short of traitorous."

"Money-laundering?" I said.

"What made you think of that?" he asked, his doughy face darkening with suspicion.

Hell's bells! I said hastily, "It's what Blainey accused other people of, so I reckon he was doing it himself."

He gave me a long, thoughtful look. "Miss Kendall, you've had several interesting telephone conversations with one of Blainey's associates, Douglas O'Rourke, an Australian national also known as Dingo O'Rourke."

"You listened in on my cell phone," I said, indignant. Then it occurred to me DHS would have recorded the calls, so they'd have Dingo telling me how Blainey asked him to carry out a murder-for-hire.

The same thing had occurred to Ariana. She pointed out how we needed the police to hear Dingo's conversation with me in order to clear Quip's name.

"Quite so. Arrangements can be made. In return we expect your cooperation."

"What type of cooperation?" Ariana asked.

"We are anxious to interview Mr. O'Rourke; however, so far he has proved elusive." He checked his watch. "If he's on schedule he'll be calling Miss Kendall shortly. When he does, you are to arrange to meet with him this evening."

Indicating Morgan and Unwin, he added, "You will be perfectly safe. These highly-trained operatives will shadow you and apprehend Mr. O'Rourke as soon as contact is made."

Highly-trained? Crikey!

* * *

It was quite unnerving the way everyone sat around and watched me answer my cell phone. Dingo's voice was urgent. "Kylie? Darleen isn't herself."

"What's wrong with her?"

"I'm not sure, but she's off her tucker. Maybe she's fretting for her kennel mates..."

"That could be it."

"Or maybe she's sick. And I can't take her to a vet for treatment, not with a big reward on offer and our pictures everywhere. Darleen knows you, Kylie. You'll have to come with the Creeling woman and take Darleen back with you tonight for treatment."

"About Ariana Creeling, she's not available. She said to tell you she'd send Bob Verritt in her place. Bob is—"

"No way, Kylie! I don't care who he is, I've never heard of him. You come by yourself, then."

He asked for a description of my car and its number plate, then he reeled off directions, which I dutifully copied down. "OK," he said, "you pick me up in one hour. That should give you plenty of time. Just you, alone. And make sure you aren't followed."

I glanced over at Morgan and Unwin. I didn't have a lot of confidence in them, but the task of simply following my car, when there was no need to worry about me seeing them, wouldn't be so difficult, would it?

CHAPTER TWENTY-TWO

"Be careful," said Ariana, touching me lightly on the arm.

"Piece of cake," I said. "Dingo would never hurt me."

She flicked a glance to the other side of our parking area, where Morgan and Unwin were getting into a brown Buick sedan. "It's those two I'm worried about. Make sure you get right out of the way when they arrest Dingo."

Bob came over to us shaking his head. "They've got that vehicle packed with every bit of surveillance equipment you could imagine, but I'm not sure those guys know how to use most of it."

He clapped me on the shoulder and grinned. "Not to worry, Kylie, they've put a global positioning device on your car, so even if they lose sight of you, they'll find you again."

There'd been some debate about whether DHS would simply wait for Dingo at the rendezvous point and arrest him there, but it had been decided to let me pick him up and drive to wherever he was keeping Darleen, so that she could be taken immediately to a veterinary hospital.

I'd been quite touched by this concern for the dingo, but then Morgan had murmured that this was a public relations gesture designed to put a caring, human face on the huge bureaucracy that was the Department of Homeland Security. "The fact that we've rescued the star of *Darleen Come Home* will be selectively leaked to news media personnel," he'd said with a small, satisfied smile.

I got into my car and put down the window to say to Ariana and Bob, "Just in case something happens to me, the next scheduled dinner for Julia Roberts is Fancy Feast grilled tuna."

Bob let loose one of his braying laughs. "That cat has a dinner schedule?"

"Jules is very particular about the order in which she eats her meals. She likes variety."

"Let's roll," called one of the dark-suited DHS people—in this case a woman—left behind when the nameless head honcho departed in a black limousine with his entourage.

She came striding over to my car. "Stand back," she said to Ariana and Bob. Directing her attention to me, she asked, "Do you have any questions pertaining to Operation Dingo before the mission is initiated?"

"Not a sausage?" I said.

"There's a problem with a sausage?"

"No prob. I mean I have no questions."

She gave me a long, suspicious stare. "This isn't a game, you know. It's a matter of national security."

She waited until I nodded solemnly, then she checked her watch. It had many dials and bristled with knobs for different functions. She raised her arm so Morgan and Unwin in the Buick could see her signal. "On my mark...Initiate!"

"You mean go?"

"Get the hell out of here!" she yelled at me.

I got the hell out.

* * *

Dingo had given me the intersection of two suburban streets in Sherman Oaks as our meeting point. I wasn't crash-hot at reading an LA street directory, but this wasn't going to be hard to find, as it was just off Ventura Boulevard, a main traffic route. All I had to do was take Laurel Canyon Drive over the hill into the Valley and when I reached Ventura Boulevard turn left. I'd zoom along for a couple of kilometers, then turn right onto a side street. Simple, really.

I lost sight of the brown Buick almost immediately, but that wasn't a worry. Morgan and Unwin knew exactly where I was heading, so even they couldn't lose me. And even if they did, the global positioning device on my car would indicate exactly where my car was.

It was Thursday night, and the traffic was horrendous. There'd been an accident on Laurel Canyon, and with no alternative route available, I had to crawl along stop-and-going with everyone else. I turned the radio on to a news station where traffic reports were given every few minutes, and was advised by a jolly-voiced announcer to avoid Laurel Canyon at all costs. "Too late, mate," I told him.

At this rate I was going to be cutting it fine with Dingo. Things improved once over Mulholland Drive, however, so if I drove fast from now on, I'd make it in time. I kept glancing up at the mirror to see if the Buick was in sight, but it didn't appear.

There was another car crash on Ventura Boulevard, where someone had run a red light, but this had just happened, so I was at the head of the jam and wasn't held up very long. There was only light traffic once I turned off onto the suburban streets. I arrived with a sigh of relief at the rendezvous point with a couple of minutes to spare.

Dingo was rapping at the passenger-side window before I'd completely stopped the car. I unlocked the door and he tumbled in. "Get going," he said. "Drive straight ahead then take the second left. Don't signal."

"How's Darleen?"

"Not too bloody good." He twisted around to check the traffic behind us. I looked up at the mirror. No Buick in view, just a couple of cars and one of those Vespa motor scooters that soaring petrol prices had made popular again.

Satisfied, Dingo turned back to the front. "A right turn coming up, Kylie, then a quick left." He indicated a driveway beside a modest little house. "Park in the garage."

As the garage door closed behind us, Dingo said, "This house is owned by a friend of a friend. He's overseas, so no worries about anyone dropping in on us."

A door led directly into the house. I followed Dingo through to the kitchen, where Darleen was lying on a bed made of several folded blankets. She sat up when she saw me, a wary look in her eyes.

"G'day, Darleen," I said. She obviously recognized me, because she relaxed enough to come over for a pat.

"See what I mean?" said Dingo. "She's not herself." He unlocked the back door. "Want some fresh air, girl?"

Darleen looked fine to me, but maybe a little down in the mouth." She could be depressed," I said.

He heaved a sigh. "It breaks my heart to let Darleen go, but I can't take chances with her health. There's any number of twenty-four-hour animal hospitals. Promise me she'll see a vet tonight."

"I promise," I said, secure that it was the truth. As soon as Morgan and Unwin arrested Dingo, Darleen would be on her way to veterinary care.

Darleen, who'd been heading for the back yard, suddenly halted. The hair rose on her neck and she gave a low growl. "What's wrong, girl?" Dingo asked her.

"That would be me," said Norris Blainey, stepping through the door. In his skinny fingers the gun looked huge. It was a wicked looking black automatic that seemed to shimmer with menace.

Darleen's growl turned into a full-fledged snarl.

"If that animal goes for me I'll put a bullet between its eyes." Dingo grabbed Darleen's collar. "Don't hurt her."

Blainey gestured with the gun. "Get back." He shut the door behind him. "I haven't time to waste. Give me the audio tape, Dingo."

Dingo's face settled into an obstinate scowl. "Go to hell."

Where were Morgan and Unwin? Weren't they supposed to be riding to the rescue right about now?

"How did you know we were here?" I asked.

Blainey's face was full of sneering amusement. "With the right equipment it's almost too easy. I've been monitoring your calls. When Dingo was giving you directions, he was giving them to me, too. Once you picked him up, all I had to do was follow you here. You never even saw me."

"The motor scooter?"

"Sharp of you. I turned off the Vespa's light and drove on the sidewalk."

Blainey's smug smile at his own cleverness was too much for Dingo. "Get out of here, you conceited bastard."

In an instant, Blainey's expression changed to one of gleeful malevolence. I felt the hair rise on the back of my neck. I was in the presence of undiluted evil.

"Over the years," he said, "I've been accustomed to paying big bucks to make certain problems go away. Since I've taken things into my own hands I've been having so much fun. And it has the added advantage that sons of bitches like you, Dingo, can't blackmail me."

"Fucking hell?" said Dingo, "you killed Yancy Grayson yourself."

"I did, with the greatest of pleasure. And in the process, killed two birds with one stone. I got rid of an employee who betrayed me, plus I set up as the murderer a talentless would-be writer who was aiming to defame me. I call that a good night's work, don't you?"

With a sickening shock, I faced the horrible reality that Norris Blainey would never have gloated over murdering Yancy unless he intended to kill us all—me, Dingo, and Darleen.

I glanced at Dingo, glowering beside me. To fuel his anger, I said, "He's going to kill Darleen."

Dingo stiffened. "What?" Still holding Darleen's collar, he took a step towards Blainey. "Not Darleen! She's just an innocent dingo." Darleen strained forward, her lip rising as she snarled.

Blainey took a step back. "Give me the audio, and maybe I won't kill her."

Dingo shook his head.

"I'll start with her front paws. A bullet in each. She'll scream, she'll howl, but she won't die. Now where is it?"

Where are Morgan and Unwin?

"Bloody hell," I hissed to Dingo. "We'll have to do it ourselves. Let Darleen go."

"But—"

"He's going to kill the three of us, anyway."

"Not my Darleen!"

With a roar of fury, Dingo released Darleen and flung himself at Blainey. She got there first, leaping at Blainey's throat. He screamed as he went down. The roar of the gun was deafeningly loud. Darleen yelped. Bright blood sprayed across the floor.

In a frenzy of rage, Dingo picked Blainey up from the floor and smashed him against the wall.

As I rushed to pick up the gun, I became aware that there was a loud thumping at the back door. The lock finally gave way and Morgan and Unwin half fell into the kitchen.

"Homeland Security. Department of Homeland Security," bellowed Unwin. "Put your hands where we can see them."

"My heroes," I said. "Just in time."

CHAPTER TWENTY-THREE

Homeland Security took most of the credit for Norris Blainey's apprehension—Dingo got some—and all of the credit for beloved dingo Darleen's safe return. This was even though Morgan and Unwin had appeared when the party was almost over. "Strewth," I said to them, "we could have been killed. Where were you?"

They had the grace to be embarrassed. Apparently they'd been held up in traffic and arrived late at the rendezvous, so they had to rely on the global positioning device to locate my Toyota. Unfortunately both Morgan and Unwin mistakenly believed the other was an expert in operating the system, so it took several frantic phone calls before they got it right.

Kendall & Creeling received no public recognition for the part we'd played, although I did get a letter of mild appreciation from the director of the whole shebang, thanking me in vague terms for my contribution to the security of the United States.

Bellina Studios and Earl Garfield decided that Dingo O'Rourke's snatching of Darleen could be a valuable PR item to promote *Darleen Come Home*, if Dingo were to be portrayed as a hero, saving the dingo he loved from death at great personal cost to himself.

When Darleen leapt for Norris Blainey's throat, the wild shot he'd made had removed the tip of her left ear, a wound that had splattered blood across the floor and ignited Dingo's overwhelming rage. Darleen herself took the injury in her stride—if she'd been able to talk, she would have said with fortitude, "This? It's nothing. Just a scratch."

Apart from being indicted for Yancy's murder, Norris Blainey was facing multiple federal charges, and his firm had slid into bankruptcy, so our premises and the rest of the block were saved from development.

Quip was healing rapidly and regaining his good looks, which cheered him almost as much as the substantial advance he got from a New York publishing company for his forthcoming book, *Norris Blainey: A Colossus Falls*.

Fran was Fran, which meant her usual grim persona was much in evidence. She did go so far as to give me a hug—an astonishing once-in-a-lifetime experience, and thank me for my help in saving Quip from murderer's row.

Lonnie confided in me that Pauline was rather taken with his new, romantic self, although a problem loomed, as Unity and Upton were coming to see him as a rival for Pauline's affections. Lonnie stoutly said he'd cross that canine bridge when he came to it.

Pauline herself scored a full-page article in the Calendar section of the *LA Times*, when to the shock and envy of the star wrangling world, she managed to get Earl Garfield to appear, if only fleetingly, at an event Glowing Bodies was coordinating for the launch of an environmentally friendly pickup truck.

In fact, thanks to Lonnie, I, along with Melodie, Lexus, and Brucie, scored invitations to the function. It was an amazing evening—never before had I seen quite so many anorexic female bodies wearing miniscule outfits and dazzling, dentally perfect smiles. The men, including Brucie, all looked mega-casual, as if they'd just this moment picked up the nearest items of clothing and thrown them on.

Two weeks after Blainey's arrest, Cousin Brucie took me to dinner. Over the main course, he leaned forward earnestly to say, "Kylie, I know you'll be disappointed, but I've got to go back to Oz. Nigel's taking advantage of Mum. I have to be there to stop it before it gets out of hand."

"I completely understand. Your mum must come first."

Brucie patted my shoulder consolingly. "Don't worry Kylie. I'll be back."

As for my mum, Jack was out of bed and taking an interest in the running of The Wombat's Retreat, but as Mum said, "He's not up to full speed yet, darl. And that's a mercy."

* * *

When I'd come back from the confrontation with Blainey, Ariana had greeted me with warm relief. Since then, however, she'd been pleasant but remote. I knew she was working through issues to do with Natalie, but I ached for the closeness we'd had, however fleeting it had been.

Several weeks passed. Bob and I were in Ariana's office, lingering after our fortnightly staff meeting, when Bob said, "I saw Dingo O'Rourke being interviewed on *ET* last night. He was talking about Darleen's rescue. Unlike Homeland Security, he gave you full credit, Kylie."

"Dingo and Darleen did all the hard work."

"Did you really say 'My heroes—just in time' when those bozos burst in after it was all over?"

I hadn't mentioned it to anyone, and hadn't realized Dingo had heard my sarcastic comment. "I might have said something like that."

A grin spread over Bob's face. "Ariana always says you're one of a kind, and she's oh so right. I can't imagine how we got on without you." He went off chuckling to himself.

"Bob thinks you're quite adorable," said Ariana, expressionless.

"He does?"

"And you don't know you are, which makes you even more adorable."

I felt a smile begin. "Do *you* find me adorable?"

Ariana smiled in turn. "I'm afraid so," she said.

Bella Books, Inc.

Women. Books. Even Better Together.

P.O. Box 10543
Tallahassee, FL 32302

Phone: 800-729-4992
www.bellabooks.com